MY SHANGHAI NEIGHBOURS

MY SHANGHAI NEIGHBOURS

MARCUS FEDDER

Published in 2024
By Black Spring Press
An imprint of Eyewear Publishing Limited
The Black Spring Press Group

Cover design by Edwin Smet
Typeset by Subash Raghu
Front cover illustration by Ding Zhiwen (Jing Zhang with the cellist Datiqin)
Back cover illustration by Niu Xintong (Jing Zhang on the Mobike)
Editor: Cate Myddleton-Evans

All rights reserved
© 2024 Marcus Fedder

ISBN 978-1-913606-28-2

No part of this publication may be reproduced, stored in or introduced into a retrieval system or transmitted in any form or by any means, electronic, mechanical, photocopying, recording or otherwise, without the prior written permission of the publisher.

www.blackspringpressgroup.com

Characters

Laowen	a 75-year-old former engineer
Jing Zhang	a 15-year-old cat
Lanfen	the 70-year-old wife of Laowen
Muyang	Laowen's and Lanfen's 35-year-old son
Mrs Bo	a 59-year-old staunch communist
Comrade Bo	a 69-year-old Communist Party official and Mrs Bo's husband
General Li	an 85-year-old former general called 'Da Heshang' by Liqin
Liqin	General Li's five-year-old granddaughter
Chen Zaoming	a 52-year-old mathematics lecturer
Donghai	Chen's 17-year-old son
Xiaomu	a 28-year-old Communist Party worker
Zhong	a 30-year-old biologist and Xiaomu's husband
Datiqin	a 78-year-old cellist
Ming	a former pianist
Ma	a former cellist
Xiaofan	a 33-year-old historian doing research in the Xincun

Instead of a Preface

This book is dedicated to all my real friends and former neighbours who lived in Shanghai in the same *Xincun* as me. *Xincun* means 'new village' and is something like a compound, and the Xincun where I lived was located in the heart of the former French Concession, the most beautiful part of Shanghai. When you think of Shanghai, you have a vision of miles and miles of beautiful modern or rather old and ugly high-rises and eight-lane motorways. But right in the middle of this bustling metropolis is a large area built in French style, consisting mostly of villas and other low-rise buildings from the 1920s, gardens, little cafes, restaurants, boutiques, galleries and schools. All the streets and narrow lanes are tree-lined. Old world charm, where cats thrive.

This book is pure fiction and all the characters are fictional — as is of course also the Xincun, with no link to reality. The only exception is the cat called Jing Zhang, who understands German and loves philosophy, Bach and the Beatles.

Laowen

Laowen looked at his watch as he walked out of the kitchen and up the staircase to the half landing. He always left the window open; it did not matter to him much whether it was summer or winter as the cigarettes always tasted the same. It was 11 o'clock, and therefore time for his second cigarette of the morning. He had not seen Jing Zhang, the black cat with two white paws, for a while and was wondering whether he had had an accident. Jing Zhang shared his love for solitude and also disliked his wife. At least this we have in common, Laowen thought. But Jing Zhang's sex life used to be better than his and he was probably younger, though now that Comrade Bo had taken Jing Zhang to the vet to get him castrated that was also a thing of the past. Laowen felt sorry for him.

He lit the cigarette and inhaled, filling his lungs with satisfying dense smoke. He counted slowly to twelve before he blew the smoke out of the window. Half of it came straight back in and drifted slowly up the staircase to the neighbours. Foreigners. At least one was a foreigner, German, the other one was Chinese and cute. Laowen's car was also German. He smiled, reflecting on this simple fact. He inhaled again.

Ever since the German had arrived one cold morning in February, he had been interested in him. He was working upstairs, often sitting on the terrace, smoking a cigar. Laowen pretended to hang up laundry on the terrace to watch the German. Many years ago, he was able to read German fluently but now this seemed ages ago and forgotten. It was during university time that his father had insisted he go to study in Germany as only Germany produces proper engineers. Laowen used to be an engineer. And now he could not speak anymore, neither Chinese nor German. At least not to his wife, and therefore probably he should not speak to his new neighbour either.

Fifteen years ago, he had decided to have a stroke. He had gone up the staircase to the open window and smoked a cigarette. The last one he thought, whilst exhaling. 'Go fuck yourself,' he had whispered across to his neighbour Comrade Bo who had been staring at him maliciously. He disliked most of his neighbours except for Datiqin. He flung the cigarette butt out of the window onto the grass in front of the house and went down again to his study. Six months earlier he had retired. He opened Goethe's *Faust* and started reading but had difficulty understanding the text. His wife was shouting from the kitchen. He hated the shouting and the idea of having to share a meal again in half an hour. This could not go on. He banged his head against the table but that brought no relief and finally decided to faint and fall off the chair. His head banged hard against the concrete floor.

Altogether he had spent a week in hospital, a ghastly week without cigarettes or Goethe, during which doctors and therapists came to see him and tried to talk to him in hourly shifts. He understood them well but decided not to answer except for grunting yes or no. Back home he sat for endless hours outside on the terrace, the same terrace that now belonged to the German and his Chinese partner. There he could smoke again, in silence, and read *Faust* and sometimes Kant but he realised that since he had returned from hospital, his understanding of German had deteriorated even further. Kant made no sense anymore and he just could not get interested in *Faust*. German was over.

Laowen used to be an engineer, until retirement, designing fountain pens. His favourite brand was Pelikan, the German brand, and as he decided to build fountain pens like the Germans do, he had also decided to continue studying German in order to be able to read Goethe and Kant, as he imagined German engineers do after work.

His new German neighbour looked like a Goethe reader, he thought.

Jing Zhang appeared one morning. A tiny kitten, he walked helplessly across the roof from the neighbouring house to Laowen's terrace, trying to climb onto his lap as he was smoking. Jing Zhang had totally black fur, except for two of his paws that were white. He seemed to like the smoke. Laowen lifted him up to look into his eyes. 'You look like Black Cat Detective Jing Zhang', he said in a whisper, realising immediately that he had done the one thing he had forbidden himself to do and that he had never ever done since falling off the chair: speak. Petrified, he looked around to see whether anyone had heard him, but no one was nearby. Even his awful neighbour's window was closed shut. He decided to talk to Jing Zhang and the cat closed its eyes and purred.

'Just wait,' he said, putting the cat down onto the other chair as he got up. He walked downstairs and returned with the leather-bound copy of Goethe's *Faust* and started reading. He realised he understood just as much of it as the cat, but it did not bother him. *Faust, Part II* was difficult.

Since that morning, Jing Zhang came by almost every day to pick up food and food for thought. When Laowen had finished *Faust, Part II,* he opened Kant. Nothing is better philosophy than Kant. But Jing Zhang seemed to be restless, so he got out an old copy of Heidegger.

How immensely silly this is, he thought as he was standing again at the window, smoking away. His neighbour passed by, a despicable creature. He had moved in during the time of the Cultural Revolution. That was when Laowen had lost his job at the pen factory. He had been classified a counter-revolutionary, a capitalist running dog because he had studied in Germany, and got beaten up by the mob who came and searched the houses of the Xincun. He had been living there since his childhood. His father had been a member of the Communist Party, but it did not help as Mao urged the youngsters not to spare anyone they might deem to be a rightist and thus against the revolution. Laowen was against the revolution, of course. When he looked at his books in later years, he was glad that he had managed to hide them away in the secret hole his father had dug to hide in during the war when the Japanese were occupying Shanghai. That hole was big enough to take all his books. My books' cowshed, he reflected. When, after ten years, he pushed the heavy wardrobe aside and dug up the wooden planks, a lot of the books had rotten away. His German books had survived. The pen factory rehabilitated him and he continued working, building pens. Not making pens. Building.

From a distance he could hear the voice of his wife, chatting with the neighbours. He was relieved that she had stopped talking to him when he had stopped responding to her. She genuinely believed that he had lost the ability to speak. As did everyone else in the Xincun, except for Jing Zhang.

When she walked past underneath the window where he was smoking, he looked at her and observed her head, her hair. Once upon a time, he had caressed that head. Did they have sex together or was that only in his imagination, as in reality she was having sex with his father and Comrade Bo? He sometimes was not sure anymore and preferred his blurred memories to the pain that certainty can bring. The only certainties that were pure pleasure were his cigarettes and his books. Goethe and Heidegger. Jing Zhang seemed to appreciate the concepts of *Dasein* too, the urge for belonging but in his case unrestricted by time and space. Laowen's Dasein was defined by the Xincun, Xuhui district and Shanghai. During the end of the Cultural Revolution, he briefly had to work on a farm in the North, Inner Mongolia, but managed to return after only a few months. There is no Dasein when you are doing slave labour, he had realised.

Laowen stopped reading. The German stranger had invited him to sit on the terrace with him and had offered him a cigar. Montecristo Habana. Laowen tried to inhale but had to cough. Even after years of smoking all sorts of tobacco, his lungs were too weak for the scents of a real Havana. Both men sat in silence, puffing away, watching the blue smoke rise in the still sky. Laowen hid the German books from the German neighbour, even though he looked interesting. He did not want to drop his disguise.

He did not wish to speak with his wife or the communists or any of the neighbours again. Ever. Silence is Dasein, he had realised one day as he flicked his cigarette butt at Comrade Bo, who was passing by again without looking up.

His wife called him a third time, and he decided to skip dinner. Pork again, he thought, why does she always cook pork which he hated? Probably for revenge as he could no longer express his dislike for pork verbally. Years ago, he wrote on a piece of paper 'I hate fucking pork'. She threw the paper into the bin and started cooking chicken for a while, but later reverted back to pork.

'Our son wants pork,' she had said.

He gave up fighting.

Lanfen and he had met the first time at the factory where she was a worker making pens. The nibs and also other parts. She was not a natural beauty but somehow the beauty of the pens, the delicate golden glow of the nibs, reflected upon her so that Laowen could only see the beauty of the pens in her. He introduced her to his parents, and they had dinner together. Later he remembered that she was mainly talking to his father, ignoring his mother. He did not think much about this though, until years after they had gotten married — when making love had become a duty rather than a nightly passion that nonetheless seemed to have produced one ugly dimwit son — he realised one evening that she was in bed with his father. He was supposed to be at the factory but had come home instead. He opened the door.

And left again. That night he started to smoke cigarettes. Returning to the factory, he locked himself up and finished three packs till dawn.

That was a long time ago.

He quietly left the house and took his bicycle and set off. At Xujiahui Park he had his first stop. Leaning his bike against the back of the bench, he sat down to watch the evening joggers run past. He took out his cigarettes. Here underneath the high trees, the tobacco tasted better. Fresher. A young girl ran past, listening to music through her earphones. He observed her stylish running and thought back to the days when he was running at Göttingen University in Germany. Her long legs soon took her out of sight, and he decided to wait till she would inevitably return for another round.

A Korean-looking, middle-aged man shuffled past, followed by his dog. Another faster jogger in red sneakers and Ray-Bans rushed past, overtaking the many people who were just walking and talking.

Across the street, a window lit up. He regularly used to cross the street after sitting in the park for a while and find solace in the arms of Madame Hu, who later moved to Suzhou to open a brothel over there. He missed her dearly — their talks about the past more than anything else. He wondered who was in that room, turning on the light. His cigarette had gone cold, and he decided it was time to cycle on.

Jing Zhang

On the morning after his operation, Jing Zhang could not walk. He had lost both his balls and his balance and swore eternal revenge. He was not sure yet how, but was determined to make a plan as he lay in a half stupor, slowly waking up. Comrade Bo had taken him to the vet and the man looked nice and professional. But was he ill? Bo had taken the precaution of talking to the vet in another room, as if suspecting that he'd understand. Of course he understood. Not only Mandarin but also Shanghai Dialect and German. But only Laowen and Datiqin suspected this secret. The vet had grabbed him with a firm hand and rubbed something with a nice smell on his nose and he had passed out immediately, falling into a beautiful and deep sleep. When he woke up, he was not sure what had happened to him and only gradually found out where the problem was. He was not too concerned, as his lovelife had stopped preoccupying him in the last years. Yes, he still went from time to time to the neighbouring compound where a former girlfriend of his lived in a shed, but she had also aged and so they nowadays just shared a meal. He was not interested at all in any of the younger cats, unlike Shan, his childhood friend. He tried to get up again, but again the walls started moving around and seemed to be crashing in on him. He heard Comrade Bo and Lanfen arguing in the room next door.

'What the fuck did you do? Why?' Lanfen shouted. Comrade Bo did not answer or Jing Zhang could not hear him. 'You could have killed him. An operation at his age is risky.'

At his age? Jing Zhang was not sure he shared that concern. Why did Comrade Bo do it? Probably jealousy, he thought as he had still been able to do something Comrade Bo lost the ability of doing a long while ago. That thought gave Jing Zhang some satisfaction. Lanfen entered and carefully lifted him up and walked up to the terrace, where her husband was sitting, smoking a cigarette. She placed Jing Zhang onto the chair next to Laowen. He did not hate Lanfen, even if Laowen thought so. Jing Zhang loved the smoke. The only thing better than cigarette smoke was cigar smoke. Recently, a German had moved in who was smoking cigars on the terrace. He understood the German as Laowen had been reading Goethe and German philosophy to him over all the years. The thing he did not like about *Faust* was that Mephisto was a dog rather than a cat.

'Look what I'm reading,' Laowen said in a whisper when his wife had gone downstairs again. '*Homo Deus, A Brief History of Tomorrow,* by Yuval Noah Harari.'

How can you have a history of tomorrow? Jing Zhang thought. He wished Laowen would read aloud, but figured it might be too dangerous as people might hear him.

'Just listen to this: "What do patients prefer, to have a short and sharp colonoscopy or a long and careful one...?"' Jing Zhang looked up. Laowen paused, shaking his head before continuing. '"There isn't a single answer to this question because the patient has at least two different selves and they have different interests."' Laowen paused again and looked at Jing Zhang who tried to look confused. 'I've had two colonoscopies and both were fascinating, Jing Zhang,' Laowen whispered. 'I don't think Harari ever had one as otherwise he would not talk about a "short and sharp one," as that does not exist.'

Thank God he's not a gastroenterologist, Jing Zhang thought. He was hoping Laowen would stop reading this stuff and get back to *Faust*. He had not read *Faust* for quite a while.

'Do you have two different selves?'

I have nine different lives but only one self, Jing Zhang thought, inhaling the cigarette smoke that was drifting by. One Dasein, one self. And no colonoscopy. He got up and jumped to the floor. It was still shaky but now he was able to walk again. He would take such dreadful revenge. Like administering a sharp and long colonoscopy. Comrade Bo would have regrets till the end of his life.

Lanfen

Lanfen came down from the terrace. The new German tenant had disturbed her time alone. He was sitting in front of his computer, writing away. Looking at him from the side, she thought about what she had been doing when she was his age. What was his age? Going down the staircase she smelled the foul odour of Laowen's cigarettes. At least the German had style and smoked cigars. Sometimes he smoked with his Chinese partner, which was weird, she thought. Why would a woman smoke a cigar, unless she was a Cuban revolutionary? Maybe she was a revolutionary, a Cultural Revolutionary, deep in her heart, beneath the surface of western clothes, iPhone and latest Macbook Pro. Lanfen stopped for a second to stare through the window through which Laowen had been smoking, to see whether Comrade Bo was sitting in the garden in front of his house. Bo was still good-looking, she thought, and at least he could talk, even though he loved talking Party politics. Years ago, she had read Mao's book of quotes in order to please him. She had bought it at the pen factory where she was working. It was the first and last book she ever bought and ever read. But then again, it is the only book one needs to read, she thought. Often, when her husband had been on night duty, she would sneak across to Comrade Bo and sink into his arms. Their sex was mediocre, Party stuff, she realised, but it was regular and communism is built on workers' routines. She thought she did nothing wrong, and the fact that she never got an orgasm screwing Bo confirmed her innocence. Once Comrade Bo had lost his liver his desire was gone. That was strange but OK, she thought, as she could find younger men in the Xincun.

Alas, she did not.

When these thoughts had finished, Lanfen sighed and went into the kitchen to prepare dinner. Ever since her son had left the house to work as a repair electrician for Shanghai's Metro system, she felt cooking to be an unnecessary burden. In fact, she loathed it. It was not just the cooking but the early-morning walk down the road to the vegetable shop where queues were forming even in winter already just after 6 a.m. The chatting with the neighbours who were buying the same vegetables and who loved talking about food. Next, on to the butcher to buy pork. It had become her daily act of silent revenge to buy pork. She remembered the night when Laowen pushed the piece of paper at her. 'I hate fucking pork'. And she had freaked out, hitting him over the head with a pan. The surprise when he simply got up and left. The surprise of the cat at the window which just stared at her without moving an inch. She disliked pork herself. The earthy meat her grandfather used to fry. She hated it but hated even more the thought of doing something to please her husband. For two months she forced herself to cook chicken, but then she just decided that was it. And it was pork. Till the end of their lives, even though she hated it.

I also tortured our son, she thought, but then again, who cares. He would be coming for dinner tonight. Maybe.

She had started work at the factory two years before they went out the first time. He was standing there, smiling at her, that somewhat dim-witted smile of an engineer. She observed him as she assembled the fountain pen, taking extra-long to put the golden nib into the black pen.

His father was very different, she thought. Plus he owned the house. If only she could live in that house without Laowen, but that, she realised, was proving difficult, so she decided to endure the latter to enjoy the former. She had made love with Laowen's father even before marrying. Old Laowen was experienced and knew how to please a woman. She wanted to shout so that the neighbours would show her the respect she thought she deserved, but he held his hand over her mouth. When, later, she was in bed with Comrade Bo for the first time she shouted long and loud, hoping that both Laowen and his father would hear. Not because it was pure pleasure or even pain, just rationally out of revenge, even though she could not say what for. Just revenge for being who Laowen was, for loving her once upon a time dearly and for being unable to return his love. A rich and sweet revenge she had hoped for but it was just sad. She realised she could not come even though Comrade Bo was trying hard.

When Lanfen first moved into the house, they were given a bedroom and a living room, which was luxurious. Lanfen had lived the previous two years with her mother in one single room on the outskirts of Shanghai. Her parents had moved there from the village where she grew up and where her grandfather grew vegetables for a living. Grandfather still raised pigs and she had to help with the pigs when she was young. Her parents had abandoned her, she felt, when they moved to Shanghai for work, leaving her in the village to be taken care of by the grandparents. She hated village life and hated pigs. And her parents, whom she only saw once a year at Chinese New Year when both of them would come to the village and get totally drunk during the festivities, ignoring her. When she was fifteen, she stole her grandfather's savings and started the long journey to Shanghai, taking buses and trains till she reached the outskirts. Her mother had told her of the vegetable shop where she worked; but Shanghai's outskirts are full of vegetable shops, and it took Lanfen more than a week to find her. The following year, her father died of cancer, but she felt nothing, not knowing her father at all, but her mother wept every evening when she had closed the vegetable shop. It was a friend who took her to the pen factory and got her an illegal job without a hukou on the assembly line in return for some pleasure behind the crate of vegetables when her mother was busy with customers. Lanfen learned that certain things are purely mechanical and done without emotion. But the hukou, the residence permit, was key and she needed to get married as soon as possible to get one, as otherwise she would have had to leave Shanghai as soon as her illegal status was found out. Laowen became her target.

When, newly married, she moved into Laowen's house, she was full of energy and enthusiasm and considered the place theirs. No, hers. They painted their rooms together and decided to plant flowers in front of the house. Lanfen planted sunflowers and vegetables.

'I hate to look after vegetables, as I had to all my life as a kid,' she said. 'So that's your job.' He smiled an enigmatic smile she did not wish to understand. In the evenings, she soon discovered they had little to talk about and no TV. She was tired from the factory floor and only adored Laowen's father, whose wit she tried to understand, often unsuccessfully. She nonetheless laughed heartily at his jokes. His mother seemed dull, but at least she cooked for them every evening. Dinner was late. Normally at 7 p.m. when they got home from the factory, and after dinner they had not much to talk about. She observed Laowen, how he took out his books and read. Each and every night. A world she did not understand. The only book she'd ever read was the only book she ever wanted to read. He even read in German.

And now they had a German neighbour. Lanfen still had the key to the apartment above hers and sometimes, when the German was not at home, she would sneak in just to be there, look at the way he and his partner lived, at the strange way they had decorated their flat. Paintings. He painted. She was horrified when she realised the white oil paint was still fresh and now stuck on her cardigan. Strange white and grey with lines. Was he alright? In the kitchen, they had a rice cooker and some other strange contraptions. She smelled one of them and it smelled of coffee. How she wished the German would offer her some real coffee, but when one day he did, she politely declined. Now, she was just sitting on their sofa, thinking about happiness, the happiness that had eluded her.

When their son Muyang was born, Laowen looked at him for a long time as if searching for something. She observed him from the hospital bed. Finally he hugged the baby. Only Lanfen knew who the father was. She did not tell Comrade Bo and Comrade Bo did not ask. Two weeks after giving birth, she was back at the factory and Laowen was back to reading his books; her mother-in-law took care of the little brute. Every routine continued and one day, for no reason Lanfen could think of, Laowen started smoking cigarettes.

She went into the kitchen and put the wok pan onto the fire. There was no sign of Laowen and she started washing the leeks and carrots she had bought early this morning at the vegetable shop. It was strange, whenever she entered the shop she was reminded of her mother and a pang of guilt hit her. Her mother ran a similar shop and she had not visited her much during the last years of her life, sending Muyang instead. Once a year she used to take the Metro to the outskirts. In the beginning she needed to change to a bus, but the new Metro line now had a stop nearby. High-rises had sprung up everywhere, and for years it looked like her mother was living on one large construction site. Her father died of cancer. Or was it asbestos? Despite the growing population, her mother's shop remained small. She never diversified into other products, sticking to fresh vegetables.

Lanfen only found out that her mother had died when she went to visit her again one New Year's Eve. It was cold and already dark outside, and the familiar shop had been replaced by a supermarket. She looked around and realised that nothing familiar was left. Muyang, who was accompanying her, could not explain things either even though he was supposed to have visited his grandmother regularly. It dawned on Lanfen that her son never actually went, but she kept the thought to herself, trying not to blame him. The people living in her mother's flat told her that the old lady had fallen and died in hospital, never regaining consciousness. Lanfen accepted a cigarette and gratefully inhaled the soothing smoke so that she did not have to speak. All the way back in the Metro she sat in silence, ignoring Muyang.

She chopped the leeks into the pan and cut the meat. Pork. Laowen did not turn up even when she shouted a third time.

Outside Jing Zhang was sitting on the windowsill, intently watching her movements. She placed a piece of meat in front of him. He briefly smelled it and decided to ignore it. She put the kettle onto the fire to boil water for the noodles. When she looked up again, Jing Zhang had kicked the piece of meat onto the street. She smiled. It's been a long time since I last smiled, she pondered. The chopped leaks sizzled in the pan. She took the meat and chucked it onto a plate and took it out in front of the house. The other cats would love it, she hoped.

Laowen did not return at six, or at seven. His bike was gone. Her son did not turn up either and did not call. She decided to eat alone, feeling peaceful. Stir-fried leeks, carrots and noodles in a garlic and ginger sauce. And udon noodles which she loved, as she always imagined eating earth worms, the thick and rich substance that wiggles when crushed by the tongue. When she looked up, Jing Zhang was still sitting there, observing her silently.

'Aren't you hungry?' she asked, and she wasn't sure whether the cat, barely noticeably, shook his head. 'Fish?'

His eyes followed her every move. Lanfen took yesterday's fish out of the fridge and put the small plate in front of Jing Zhang, who withdrew his front paw. After ignoring the fish till Lanfen had finished the washing up, he finally grabbed a piece delicately with his teeth and started eating.

'At least you're not throwing the plate onto the street,' Lanfen said. Comrade Bo's wife walked past.

'Fuck you old bitch,' Lanfen whispered. She hated Comrade Bo's wife, who was younger than her. Bo had moved into the Xincun during the Cultural Revolution and his wife much later, whereas her husband's family had always been living there. The Bos were usurpers who had disturbed the peace. Comrade Bo, she was told, had smashed up peoples' houses and burned books. He beat up teachers. Only later did he become quieter, and now he was wearing sweatshirts with a flag of the USA, the former arch-enemy. His wife had remained a true and loyal hardliner. Though she had been too young to be part of the Cultural Revolution, it seemed, she had never gotten over it and continued living it every day.

'Fuck you,' Lanfen said again, this time a bit louder. Jing Zhang seemed to agree, staring angrily at the disappearing figure. Lanfen smiled again.

Having done the washing up, she was unsure whether to go for a walk or even join the German neighbour on the terrace. In the end, she decided to walk a bit. Her old bones were getting arthritic from the cold during the short winters. Their flat had no heating, like most of the flats in the south of China. But she had seen the modern radiators installed in the apartment above, so the German and his partner would not suffer from the cold. As she turned into the street, she observed the traffic. Shanghai had changed so much. When she had first arrived, there were so many bicycles and so few cars. Then the bikes disappeared and there were only cars. Now the bikes had reappeared and she was counting the Mobikes in front of the entrance to the Xincun. Her son had downloaded the Mobike app onto her new smartphone, which he had given her as a present, and now she could take any bike to ride anywhere in town and just leave it standing anywhere. True communism.

She decided to walk. She knew literally everyone on the street but did not greet anyone. Only when her son's teacher walked past did she stop to say hello.

'A beautiful evening,' he said. 'But may be raining later on?' She smiled at him, remembering the one beautiful evening many years ago when Muyang was in his class in primary school. How difficult things had been for Muyang to learn to read and to write. His teacher had been so patient, teaching him calligraphy so that he would learn to differentiate the many characters which looked all the same to him. He smiled back at her and put his hand on her shoulder, touching the bones that once used to be covered with smooth skin and subtle muscles. He seemed to remember too, she thought.

'Is Muyang OK?'

'Yes, thanks for asking. He is always OK.'

'Happy bunny he always was.' He turned around and walked on. Lanfen realised how his words and the touch of his hand had suddenly let an immense sadness overcome her. She did not know why but she felt like crying, crying like a child on her grandfather's farm when she was standing there watching how a pig got slaughtered, hearing its immensely sad cries in the night. She crossed the street and saw a Western stranger light a cigarette. She had three cigarettes left and took one out. The stranger handed her a packet of matches. She inhaled.

She would never again cook pork, she decided, as she turned left into Wulumuqi Road to avoid the strangers and the shops' neon lights. Only then did she allow herself to cry.

Jing Zhang

Jing Zhang had his favourite place on the wall from which he could observe all the important windows. Lying flat on his tummy was much easier without his balls, he noticed. Some positive side effect, but he remembered that he had sworn eternal revenge nonetheless.

From the moment he could walk again, he ensured that all the cats would use Comrade Bo's garden patch for their daily business. Even he thought it stank. The cats took it in turns. When the window was open, they would pee on the sofa or on the bed. Soon the window remained shut. Jing Zhang was sitting at a safe distance observing. It seemed to take a while for Comrade Bo to realise what was happening and Mrs Bo did not seem to be around. It was deeply satisfying to see that Comrade Bo had to fix a grid to the window so that the cats would not enter anymore. Naturally, his armchair in the garden was not spared either.

Muyang

He was 21 when he left the Xincun, moving to the north of Shanghai. Well, he did not really move out as he came back most weekends. He had just got a job with Shanghai Metro, allegedly because of his father's connections, though he believed that it probably was Uncle Bo who had made the calls. Changing lightbulbs needs to be done by someone and that's how he started. But soon he felt that he could be tasked with more complex problems. Fixing the system that operates the carriage doors was left to engineers, but unblocking blocked aircons, even repairing the electronic gates was for him. But today he was replacing a number of lightbulbs again. He loved the feeling of the round glass between his fingers. One could squeeze it indefinitely without breaking it — strength, but he had no clue why, just like an egg, he thought. He took out his screwdriver and opened the cover. A long-haired girl walked past in black trousers and a white jacket. She had looked at him. Many girls look at him, because of his hairstyle. He was self-conscious but also vain enough to enjoy the attention; attention from strangers which his parents had never given him. That he was attractive to women was something he first noticed at the beginning of puberty. Mainly elderly women. The young ones at school were not interested in him and neither was he interested in them. But the older teachers and the women in the Xincun were different.

He took out the broken lightbulb and put it into the box from which he had taken the new one. Carefully, he put it in. With something which he thought sounded like 'pling', the light came on. It was most satisfying. He climbed down from the ladder, packed up and walked back to the office. He had replaced three bulbs.

He had also replaced a broken bulb at Uncle Bo's place when he was 14 or 16. Uncle Bo's wife had called him in. He had returned from school and was mucking around in the garden in front of their house, kicking a football up, counting how many kicks he could keep the ball in the air. It was a stuffy afternoon, a typical pre summer holidays afternoon. His parents were out, otherwise he would have been doing homework. He could not be bothered with school grades. Gaokao, the finals, were not even in his imagination. The main thing was to get through middle school. She called him from the window.

'Can you fix a lightbulb?' she asked. He thought he could, wiping his hands on his shorts. Her door was open and she stood in the ground floor hallway leading to their apartment. He was not sure about her age. She was wearing a long t-shirt and shorts. Small beads of sweat were running down her cheek.

'Where?' he asked, looking around.

'Let me get you a chair to climb up,' she said, closing the door. She moved a chair into the middle of the room and he climbed up. The chair was very wobbly and appeared to be falling apart any moment.

'Let me hold you so that you don't fall,' she said, grabbing his legs with both hands. He felt a strange sensation as her fingers touched his flesh. Carefully, he took out the old bulb and climbed down again to fetch the new one. The moment he had climbed up again, she held him again, this time around his hip. He felt an intensity of feelings that made it difficult to fix the new bulb. By the time he had got down again, her hands were under his shirt. She kissed him. He had never kissed before and felt her tongue and enjoyed the feeling, the intensity of the sensations, her body against his, her skin under his hands, her naked breasts. First time ever. His pants were wet even before they started making love.

'Want a Coke?' asked the foreman when he entered the station office.

'Not sure what's wrong with the current. Why did it blow out three bulbs at the same time?'

Muyang didn't know or care as he was still in his dream lying on Mrs Bo's bed, overwhelmed by the warmth both inside and out.

He put the ladder into the corner next to the coat hangers and sat down, opening the can of Coke. It was fresh and sweet. Like the drink he had after making love to Mrs Bo. He remembered that she was shouting and he was worried lest someone would hear them. But it was wonderful, both the sex and the shouting. He only left once he could smell his mother's cooking. He aimed to sneak into the house, trying to conceal the too obvious wet spot on his shorts. He was grateful that she did not say anything but also realised that she probably understood. Her attitude towards him seemed to have changed from that day. She now treated him like a man, he thought, like an adult, no longer like a child.

Listlessly he finished the Coke. Another hour and he could leave work. Another thing to fix. A turnstile this time round. He opened it up and his thoughts did not drift away. After trying out various things, he saw the loose cable and re-attached it. After 55 minutes, he had closed the turnstile and tried it a couple of times. It was working perfectly. Satisfied, he went back to change out of his work clothes, hanging his uniform on the coat hanger. One day the uniform also had a spot. It was embarrassing. He had fallen asleep and had the most beautiful dream making love to one of the European women whom he often saw passing through the station. When he awoke it had happened. His colleagues had returned and noticed. For weeks they were cracking jokes about him.

Now he was on his way home to his parents. He visited them every now and then, ideally when there was no special reason, as he hated to come back for Chinese New Year, birthdays or Mid-Autumn Festival. He walked through the gates of the Xincun, savouring the familiar smells. He was wondering whether he would encounter Uncle Bo or his wife.

Once the ice had been broken, Muyang had become a frequent visitor to Mrs Bo. He had been wondering whether Comrade Bo was leaving them on purpose so that he could do what Comrade Bo seemed incapable of doing. The intensity of after-school fucks became quite addictive and he figured that most people in the Xincun knew about it. Certainly the grey cat with strange eyes knew about it, as he often witnessed things, sitting on the windowsill at the most inappropriate moments.

Muyang passed the old cellist, Datiqin, who greeted him affectionately. Datiqin had always been his friend, even though he had to give up cello lessons after a year of trying. He could not even play the simplest scales properly, it was hopeless. His father had concluded that enough was enough and decided to teach him calligraphy instead. This decision had led to a major row between his parents, but in the end his mother gave in.

'You have much enthusiasm, but you'll never be another Yo-Yo Ma,' Datiqin had said.

That was fine, he agreed, as he went home after his last lesson. Datiqin stopped as they were nearing his house.

'How is work?' he asked.

'All well, lots to do,' Muyang replied.

'Keep it up, the Metro is amazing. The other day I read about the Underground in London. It is horrible. Dirty, hot, stuffy, too crowded.'

'Wish I could see it one day, Datiqin,' he replied with a smile. In the distance he could see a black cat with white paws observing him. He said goodbye to Datiqin in order to meet his old friend. Crouching down in front of him, he caressed his black ears. He knew he was his father's special friend and that some secret seemed to connect them. But then again, some secret had connected him also with the grey cat who had always watched him making love to Mrs Bo. He had taken the grey cat along to his new place when he moved out, but, sadly, the cat ran away. He agreed, his tiny moist room in the basement of a high-rise was not the same as Xincun life.

He could smell his mother's cooking, but then his mobile rang. He decided to see his parents another day.

Jing Zhang

This was terrible, Jing Zhang realised, when he saw a little girl leaving with her cello. He had been listening to the lesson and was as glad that it was over as Datiqin and the girl herself must have been. Still better than the boy practicing the hautboy on the other side of the Xincun, but, no, this girl would never be a Rostropovitch.

Datiqin had told him about Rostropovitch after he had come back from a concert. It must have been hard for him as Rostropovitch had been playing his favourite concerto, Schumann, the one you definitely need your little finger for. He had jumped onto Datiqin's lap as he sat brooding, smoking a cigarette. Funny that humans are so often brooding. And smoking cigarettes.

As the little girl left the house, Jing Zhang sneaked into Datiqin's room.

'So, here you are. Hmm. That was terrible, wasn't it.'

Jing Zhang agreed, jumping onto the bookshelf from where he had a better view. Datiqin took his cello and started playing the Gigue of the third Bach suite. Jing Zhang knew it by heart. He liked listening to the cello. Of all the musicians and their instruments in the Xincun, the cello was the one he liked most and Datiqin was his favourite musician. The two seem to go together, he realised. But does cello music produce melancholic people? He lay on his back and stretched his legs. The scars from his operation were still hurting when he stretched too much. Fuck Bo, he thought.

Jing Zhang used his ingenuity to punish Bo. Not only did the cats do their business on Bo's front steps and in his garden, but he also got them to carry old fish heads from the restaurant opposite and deposit them on his doorstep and on the windowsill. In the cavity of the wall, he pushed pieces of ham which Lanfen had left for the cats of the Xincun. The ham would soon rot and attract the wasps. Ham left at door level was for the rats. Jing Zhang felt smug when he had completed the tasks. He would return in a few days to watch how things developed.

When Datiqin had finished the Gigue, Jing Zhang got up and jumped down to the floor to head for the door which Datiqin opened for him.

'Not staying today?' He wasn't sure why but today did not seem to be Datiqin's day. His cello playing was also pretty bad — he had heard better Gigues before. Maybe also Datiqin was getting old, Jing Zhang thought. He scratched on General Li's door, but Li wasn't at home.

He decided to visit Laowen on the terrace but only found the German working on his computer, who looked up and smiled. Jing Zhang rubbed against his legs. Corduroy trousers. He jumped up to sit on his lap. Would he smoke a cigar? But the German continued typing on his computer without smoking, stroking Jing Zhang's neck from time to time. There are worse ways to spend an afternoon, he thought as he dozed off.

Mrs Bo

The one who wins is not the one with better arguments but the one who can more convincingly swear unswerving loyalty to Chairman Mao. This long thought exhausted her.

'I can,' she said, looking at herself in the mirror, seeing the face that was showing this subtle sadistic smile. And I am more convincing. Still glancing at the face in the mirror, she saw Comrade Bo through the door to the bedroom. 'Old fart,' she whispered with contempt. The man that once was. She finished putting on the make-up that covered the wrinkles around her eyes and drew two long black lines where her eyebrows should have been. Her best days were clearly past, a fact that did not prevent her from looking down on other people whose best days were also clearly past.

The best days were during the Cultural Revolution. And how she regretted not having been an active part of it. From her husband's stories, this was the time China could have been saved, just when the final victory over the revisionists and rightists was close. Alas. She was six when it all started and remembered the excitement when the hordes of pupils from her school, barely older than she was but with bright red armbands, beat up the teachers and ransacked the classrooms. For a moment she was speechless when they tore all their paintings from the classroom walls. Even her own painting that she had so beautifully painted with black ink, with brush strokes that spread over the rice paper as if by themselves. There it was, lying on the floor, being trampled on by the dirty shoes of some 16-year olds. She had tried to save it, but it was in vain; instead, she stamped on it herself to show her allegiance to a cause she could not comprehend.

When she got home, her mother was cooking as if nothing had happened. They were living in a small town far from any university and it had taken some time for the revolution to spread beyond third-tier cities. A month later, she saw her father being paraded through town as if he was a criminal. She ran up to him but was torn away by a girl who was trying to look important. She kicked the girl but was beaten in return. Her father ignored her. A week later he came home and life continued and her father resumed his life as a simple policeman. But school did not continue, and the 16-year-olds did not go back to the classroom. Later, she realised that a number of teachers never returned. Some had taken their lives, others got killed, others were still working in mines up north. Rightists, serves them right. By the time she was 16, Chairman Mao was preparing the meetings with President Nixon, the arch-enemy, the devil personified, and mysteriously, the revolution had stopped. In her head, it did not stop. Why would it, it was not finished. But everything else in her head had stopped a long time ago. School, reading, learning. She found solace in her work in the local factory producing bicycle frames, in the monotony of the movements, tightening the screws for which she did not need to think a lot. The movement taking over the thinking, the repetition planting itself in her brain so that it would continue even after work. When she got home after a long day, more dreariness awaited her. To join the Communist Party, she started studying the writings of Chairman Mao. Whilst her colleagues were progressing on to read Lenin and then Marx, she continued reading Mao. One day, only one other person was at the meeting. She looked up from her book and saw Hu, whom she had seen at the other assembly line. Hu seemed shy but now he smiled. She returned the smile as there was not much else she could do and both of them decided to go out. Passing the dark factory office, Hu checked the door. It yielded. He pulled her into the room and immediately started kissing her. So he was not that shy after all, she realised. Mrs Bo had only a few times before touched another man, or, rather, been touched by another man. The first time, one Chinese New Year when they were visiting her father's parents in the village, her uncle had dragged her into the barn, torn down her underwear and immediately did the unthinkable. It had hurt like hell and she had tried to fight, but he was much stronger. In the end she had yielded. When it was over, she felt a mixture of shame and disgust but did not tell her parents or anyone. The next day her father took her home again. She was barely 14. The following year, she sought out her uncle's son who was two years younger than her and seduced him so that her uncle could hear. She thought it was revenge but was annoyed when her cousin seemed to enjoy it. So when Hu started kissing her, she knew what to do and tore open his shirt and pulled down his trousers. He seemed taken aback by her sudden action but in the end, they made love. That is, she made love to him whilst he remained passive and perplexed. Two weeks later they set off for Shanghai to visit Hu's uncle.

At first she felt this huge city numbed her senses. The noise, the traffic, the dirt were overwhelming and different. They were living with Hu's uncle in the basement of a high-rise. His uncle was guarding a factory at night, and so they could sleep in the only bed but had to vacate it when he came back at 7 a.m. Hu soon found a job taking over the day shift from his uncle which meant that Mrs Bo could simply stay in bed, which suited her better as getting up at 7 a.m. was too harsh. And Hu's uncle could do what he had been dreaming about but had failed to accomplish. It felt horrible, she thought, but so what. She helped out in a local shop, a job she disliked. She wanted to be a Communist official, not so much because she understood what it meant but because she saw them driving past in black limousines.

After two months she had had enough and remembered Chairman Mao's book and set off to discover true revolution in the mega city. The district office of the Communist Party was surprised when she applied for a job, appearing out of nowhere, and basically told her to get stuffed. She had no Shanghai Hukou, the residence permit you need to be a person in the city. She left the Party building disillusioned, and returned to

Hu's uncle who was sitting at the porch chatting to a friend. The friend told her to go to Jianguo Road as the Xincun was looking for a junior to help in the Xincun's Party office.

She left a note to Hu that she would not be back and took bus No 377 to Jianguo Road. The bus was full of old people who seemed to have nothing to do. She despised the look of them but also despised herself for having to travel on the same bus as them. Once she had risen up the ranks, she would have a car and a chauffeur, she was sure. On Wulumuqi South Road she got out. A guy, probably ten years older than her, was standing at the bus stop, smoking a cigarette. He was reasonably good-looking.

'Can I borrow one?' she asked.

Looking surprised, he gave her a cigarette. She inhaled and coughed violently.

'First time?'

'Yeah,' she lied. He smiled at her.

'New here?'

'No.'

It was evident the guy did not believe her.

'Where are you off to then?'

'Xincun,' she said. The guy looked at her.

'Well, that's where I live. Who are you looking for?'

'The Party office.'

'Hmm. Let me take you there,' he grunted. 'I'm Bo, by the way.'

I'm Bo, by the way. Those fateful words.

She looked again at the mirror where Comrade Bo had just been a reflection in the glass as he was walking by. Had their relationship always been like that, a reflection in a dirty mirror? Mrs Bo looked at herself again, trying to adjust the lines that were to resemble her eyebrows. Her hand seemed to be slightly trembling and she was not sure whether it was due to age, a lack of sleep or Parkinson's. She feared Parkinson's.

Everyone feared Parkinson's. Mrs Bo was part of a group of elderly women, all Party activists. The group used to meet in person but now their interaction was mainly on WeChat. In the beginning, they used to discuss the writings of Chairman Mao; but now it seemed that their interest in politics had faded, and she received mainly short video clips with cooking advice and self-care tips from Traditional Chinese Medicine. She herself sent out many posts about Parkinson's and how to treat it, hoping to receive more information back. Many of the women were also too absorbed with their duties as grandparents. It bored her to death. She had no children.

When, after seven years, Mrs Bo had finally gone back to her hometown to visit her parents, her father had Parkinson's and her mother had been killed by a motorcycle. Thank God the motorcyclist had not survived either. She went to the local temple and burned bags and bags of spirit money for her mother, trying unsuccessfully to feel low for not visiting her whilst she was still alive. You are supposed to look after your parents when they reach old age, but Mrs Bo loathed them. So no visits on New Year's Day. The burnt money would compensate and would make her mother's life under the ground more pleasant. She felt no emotion at all. And she knew that soon she would be burning another stash of spirit money, fake banknotes, for her father.

'Fucking keep the money for him, so that I don't need to come back and do it again,' she shouted at her mother's spirit, hoping to be heard. There was no answer, which did not really surprise her. As a Communist Party official, you were supposed to be a materialist with zero superstition. But what if Marx, Lenin and Mao had been wrong and the afterworld existed? Back in Shanghai, she continued burning fake bank notes but in temples that were far enough away where she could be sure nobody knew her. She was happy to find a pile of fake dollar notes which she burned too, just in case.

Later when she had returned to the office, she smelled of smoke but her boss did not ask any questions. Mrs Bo figured she knew, as in fact everyone knew, and everyone hedged their bets by praying to the gods and the spirits and to their ancestors in the temples. Everywhere in the country.

The Party office in the Xincun had turned her down. No hukou, and without a hukou, the residence permit everyone needs, she was a nobody. She was expected to leave but remained seated.

'I'm not going anywhere.'

'You can be the janitor, but don't tell anyone. There is a room at the end of the Xincun, next to the bicycle shed. That's where you can live.'

She accepted without inspecting the place. It was better than going back to Hu and his uncle or home and she would try to stay as much as possible with Comrade Bo. She soon discovered that sex with Bo was better than with those two she had left behind.

Three months later, she married Comrade Bo and moved into the Xincun officially. Now she was someone, as Comrade Bo was someone. Now she got a hukou. Now she could look down on the neighbours. None was a true revolutionary, none a communist. Probably all rightist roaders who survived, she thought.

'I'll get them all,' she muttered in the mornings when she looked into the mirror before heading off to work. Work. Now it was clear that, even though she was the junior, she would not do any cleaning jobs herself. But she had to make sure that the garbage collection was properly organised. That the paths and the lawns were clean. She shouted at her neighbours for dropping cigarette butts. But when she smoked she simply dumped hers in the grass when she was sure nobody was looking.

To her regret, the Communist Party did not provide her with a car. She never progressed from her initial job.

Recently, one person had caught her attention in the Xincun. An elderly man who appeared most arrogant, ignoring her. He had moved in only three years ago. She represented the Communist Party and the Party demanded respect. He had none. And, worse, he was joined by a four-year-old girl who followed her grandpa's example and ignored Mrs Bo. The brat secretly stuck out her tongue.

Mrs Bo told the girl off, but that did not change the behaviour as her grandpa stoically walked on, ignoring her and her reprimands. Then one day, Mrs Bo managed to catch the girl dropping an ice cream wrapper on the ground, next to the bench where she was sitting with her grandpa who was reading a newspaper.

'Pick it up,' demanded Mrs Bo with a stern voice. The girl stuck out her tongue and continued serenely licking her ice cream. 'Pick it up, you little brat,' she demanded again. Nothing happened and her grandpa briefly glanced up from behind the newspaper and then continued reading, totally ignoring her. No, not her, he ignored the Party.

Enraged, Mrs Bo tried to slap the girl but did not succeed as General Li quickly blocked her arm. Without thinking twice, she kicked him instead. It must have hurt. She paused, and there was silence. General Li continued reading as if nothing had happened. Mrs Bo retreated, unsure of what to do next.

The next week she was fired from her job in the Xincun's Communist Party office. She handed back the keys and cleaned out her desk. Back home, she felt ashamed in front of Comrade Bo who remained silent for a while.

'You obviously don't know who he is.'

Mrs Bo shook her head.

'General Li. His father fought with Chairman Mao. Long March. Everything. He is a princeling. Be careful who you pick a fight with.'

'Fuck.' She paused, not understanding her husband's words. 'What's a princeling?'

'You illiterate idiot,' Bo said with contempt. 'A son or daughter of Chairman Mao's closest comrades. Li's father was with Mao from the very start.'

'Fuck.'

Mrs Bo lit a cigarette and left the house. A general and a princeling on top of that. How stupid of her not to know who he is. But then again, how unusual of a general to live a simple life in the Xincun, like everyone else. She thought all Party princelings would live in luxury and not amongst normal people. If she were a princeling, she knew where she would live. Not here. Alas, she was still a normal mortal, particularly now that she had been fired from her job.

To her great annoyance, General Li saw her the next evening in the shop where she was buying beer for Bo and herself. He slowly walked up the aisle towards her, and she was prepared to be hit as he lifted his hand — but he gently put his hand onto her arm and just shook his head.

'You demand respect but show none for the elderly nor for children for that matter. Go and read Confucius. Be humble,' he said quietly. She looked at his hand and then at her own where her fingers were shaking.

She rushed out of the shop without saying anything and turned into Wulumuqi South Road where she stopped. Confucius. She had heard of him but never read any of his writings. She felt immensely low and barely managed to light a cigarette.

Over the next days, she mostly slept. What is life now about, if the meaning of life was taken away? It seemed the meaning of life consisted only of the meagre content of her office drawer. Mrs Bo found another job in the nearby post-office on Hengshan Road. She had difficulty with numbers but, in the end, managed to finish every day half-way intact. Comrade Bo was often late, and she waited for him in the kitchen. Waiting without hope, smelling the stench of the burning fat in the pan.

Her thoughts drifted back to the time when the boy from next door appeared in front of her window.

'Hey, Muyang,' she shouted. 'Can you help me fix a lightbulb?'

He came over and climbed up the chair to reach the lamp hanging from the ceiling. She held him as he was balancing, reaching for the bulb. A long-forgotten feeling reappeared. She held him steady and realised how his trousers were bulging. 'He's too young,' said a voice inside her. He held on to her shoulder, climbing down, and she drew him closer to herself, excited by the softness of his skin.

This was so wrong, she thought to herself, lying on the bed, smoking a cigarette when Muyang had gone. But it was fun, albeit far too fast and short. Youth has no stamina. Men on the long march must have been different. She stretched out her arms to observe her hands, which were beautiful. Quickly she got up, tidied the bed and prepared dinner for Comrade Bo who would be coming home soon.

Thoughts of the past always pleased Mrs Bo. The past was not as unpleasant as others remember it to have been. Her childhood was wonderful as it happened in the middle of the Cultural Revolution. Years with minimal schooling, years of revolutionary slogans.

Gradually her thoughts resurfaced to the present. She lit another cigarette, observing her face in the mirror. Suddenly she saw Jing Zhang. He was staring at her through the window, as if able to read her thoughts. Too much. She closed the curtains. In the room next door, she could hear Comrade Bo starting the stereo. That was one thing both still had in common: the secret love for western music, in addition to revolutionary songs. About five years ago, Comrade Bo had managed to buy a pile of old vinyl with rock and roll music. He put on Dire Straits. 'There's a shiver in the dark and it's raining in the park…' Mrs Bo left the bathroom and entered the living room. There Comrade Bo was sitting, bent over the vinyl player. He did not want to buy CDs. What had become of Hu? she suddenly thought.

She looked at her husband, crouched over the music player. So, that's Bo by the way, she thought. That's what is left of Bo, by the way. Communism gone, liver gone, prostrate operation, probably cancer, no desire to fuck, but still loving rock and roll. And still she loved him, she thought, and went over to hug him. He got up to face her and held her in his arms. His cheek tasted slightly salty.

Jing Zhang

Jing Zhang had developed a sense for situations he knew he should not be watching. Like when Comrade Bo had inadvertently locked him into the bathroom and he had to endure observing Bo analyse his haemorrhoids. Not a pretty sight, he thought, Karma hits you in all sorts of weird places. That was long before he got castrated. He knew that Bo's sex-life was non-existent and had in a way pitied him for this. He knew from looking through various windows that Mrs Bo quite happily enjoyed other men's beds, but from another old cat he had learned that also Comrade Bo had previously had neighbourly relations which were beyond his job description as a Party secretary.

'Oh well, not all humans can be monogamous,' that old cat had concluded.

'As if you were,' had been his answer, but the cat had already walked away.

And now he felt some inner satisfaction. At least Bo could not do what he could no longer do.

Comrade Bo

'Part of your prostate had to be removed,' said the surgeon, leaning over Comrade Bo. 'Without your prostate gland or seminal vesicles you will no longer experience ejaculation.'

Bo saw the surgeon's face disappearing, and a deep fog seemed to be drifting through the oxygen supply into the room, covering the doctors and nurses around his bed. From the distance, a voice continued like a robot. He picked up words like 'erectile dysfunction.' Lack of lust. Hunger. Safety. He did not want safety, he thought as the fog turned dark grey, like smoke from a fire.

Three days later, his wife pushed his wheelchair back through the Xincun. He tried to gauge whether his neighbours were showing any Schadenfreude. He would have understood. Now was their moment of revenge, revenge by smiling at him, by offering nice words of condolence. But no one would ever know what really had happened. He had sworn the surgeon to secrecy.

'Yeah, liver,' he said when asked. And everyone nodded in sympathy. If only they knew. Deep inside, he feared that if they knew they would no longer take him seriously. A communist who has erectile dysfunction? Unthinkable. Chairman Mao was known to enjoy life to the fullest even in old age and he, Bo, would …

Shit, this was too horrible to contemplate.

Bo barely managed to climb out of the wheelchair on his own and simply dropped onto the bed. It was just all so fucking depressing, he thought, lighting a cigarette.

A boy was staring at him through the open window. Muyang, their neighbours' son.

'Go fuck yourself, you little brat,' he shouted. He secretly quite liked the little brat who was leading an insufferable life with his imbecile father and the mother Bo used to fuck. Did Muyang know who his real father was? It did not matter, he thought as Muyang's face disappeared and he could hear the football bouncing off the wall of the other house.

He did not really trust his neighbours, and his neighbours definitely did not trust him. He was a newcomer to the Xincun even though he had been living here since 1970.

Comrade Bo was a big-wig revolutionary Red Guard, age 20. He had joined the Red Guards right at the beginning in 1966 and made his name ransacking houses in the former French concession, smashing other peoples' furniture and, what he liked best, the occasional porcelain collection. He loved the sound when the fine bone china crushed under his shoes, his Jiefang xie, which means 'liberation shoes,' which he as a Red Guard wore with pride. Crushing delicate porcelain caused pain on the owners' faces as if he had crushed their toes. And yet he was smart. He was always the first in the study, searching for money hidden in the obvious places, behind books, in vases. Most people have similar hiding places, he discovered. He never took jewellery, though. Whilst leaving his co-revolutionaries to smash up glass and furniture, he would quickly hide the money in the lining of his pants. Getting caught would have meant getting lynched or the death penalty, he knew only too well as his closest friend was shot in prison the other day. Comrade Bo was undeterred, and no one challenged his authority as he was the loudest and the most brutal. He would have liked to be called daring, but his friends knew just as well as him that to be a thug was the opposite of daring. To crush porcelain and beat up people in their houses in the former French concession was not particularly heroic or communist.

One evening, he remembered, he had found a pile of vinyl in the study of an elderly lady. He could not read the covers and had no idea that the pictures on the covers were of a piano or violin. Together with the books, he threw the vinyl through the window into the garden, ready to be burned. The old lady sat ash-faced, watching him. He ignored her — she was a bloody counter-revolutionary who would keep China in serfdom and the workers oppressed. One cover looked different from the others. The woman raised her arm. 'Don't. Not this one, please.' He was surprised and looked at the woman who had been watching the destruction of her home without saying anything. He had dropped a white and blue vase. She had not flinched.

'It was a birthday present from my father.'

'As if the revolution cares,' Comrade Bo shouted at her. But he put the vinyl aside. Later he hid it underneath his coat and when he had reached his room he hid it underneath his bed, folded in an old winter coat the previous owners had left behind. He did not know why he had taken it or what to do with it but instinctively felt it was forbidden. Lying on his bed, he felt a sense of deep satisfaction. Defiance and Destruction.

The stolen money he hid underneath the floorboards.

When he was 20, he had been given two rooms in the Xincun. That was in 1970. The owners were counter-revolutionary capitalists. The wife was in jail, the husband sent to work on a farm in Inner Mongolia. He was grateful that the guards had only done a half-hearted job. The furniture was intact, the bed comfortable with a real western mattress. Utter luxury, he thought, realising he liked it. When he moved in, he saw the hostile glances of the neighbours but did not care. They seemed to despise him for being a newcomer, and gradually he discovered that most of them had already been living there when they were children. The Xincun had been built for the employees of an insurance company and most of the locals were bourgeoisie. Rightist roaders.

When he was 18, he had been called upon to help as the Red Guards were finally closing down the Shanghai Conservatory. It was known for being a hotbed of western decadence, teaching western music played on western instruments. He walked down the corridor, kicking doors open. Behind one door a young professor, barely older than himself, was sitting waiting for what would happen. Cello. Comrade Bo had no idea what a cello was. The room was empty, as if cleaned up prior to their arrival. He was looking for musical instruments in the wardrobes but could not find anything. Getting angry, he shouted at the professor to get up.

'Where are your fucking instruments?'

'There are none.'

'Liar,' he shouted. He hit the professor over the head and took a heavy book from the shelf and threw it at him. It hit him in the stomach, and he stumbled backwards and fell onto the chair. Bo grabbed his hand to pull him up, but the professor's hand was soft and offered no resistance. Bo got furious as the hand slipped out, holding on to his little finger he twisted it. There was a crack when the finger broke, but no noise came out of the professor's mouth. Bo pushed him back onto his chair and left the room to continue the search for forbidden instruments in the next rooms along the corridor. He found cellos and violins hidden in the attic and burned all of them in a huge fire in the courtyard. Amazing satisfaction, particularly as they forced the professors to watch the fire.

That evening he was thinking back to the professor. He was surprised at his stoicism, his unflinching face when he had broken the little finger. The helplessness of the finger dangling loose from the hand. One voice inside him made him feel mean and inhuman. The other told him that this was the price of being a counter-revolutionary. Bo decided to listen only to the latter voice. It took another six years until the former voice had the upper hand, but by then breaking fingers was no longer an acceptable means of dealing with the bourgeoisie. It was bad luck that he ended up living in the same Xincun as the cellist.

It was only many years later that he saw in a second hand shop a weird contraption.

'A record player,' said the owner, putting a record on. It started turning and music came out of the side.

'Wait, don't sell it,' Comrade Bo said. He rushed home and found the vinyl in a pile of old clothes underneath the bed. He was glad he had taken it along when he had moved into the Xincun. He went back and asked the shopkeeper to play it, watching how he carefully took the vinyl out of its cover. He put the needle down and heard a scratching sound. And then music — a male voice singing 'While My Guitar Gently Weeps'.

He did not understand the verse and just listened to the music.

'Beatles,' said the shopkeeper. Bo nodded but had no clue what that meant. He bought the record player. Every evening he played the music, listening to the lyrics he did not understand. Mrs Bo had little understanding of music but tolerated it. This song would remain his favourite. The music was so different from the revolutionary music he was used to. Western music was decadent and oppressive. But why? He agreed to disagree, which was rare, as he normally agreed with all Party policies and statements, even when they changed in tone and character from Mao to the Gang of Four during the Cultural Revolution to Comrade Deng after the Revolution.

Bo adored President Xi.

It was only in 2018, when he saw the new foreign neighbours who were living above Laowen and Lanfen, that he had his first real contact with foreigners. Yes, he had said hello to foreigners as part of his Party work, and had seen them walking down Huahai Middle Road, or hanging out at Zapata's on Hengshan Road, but he had never ever talked to them as he had adhered to old-school thinking, branding foreigners as evil neo-colonialists. But now there was a German and his younger Chinese partner. The German greeted him every day. His partner was called Ms Fan. He decided to call her Xiaofan, Little Fan, like all the other old people in the Xincun seemed to call her. At first, Comrade Bo ignored the German, but one day after a few weeks, when the German had offered to help him carry stuff back from the shop, Bo smiled back, surprised at himself. It took another two months of mutual smiling till he had the courage to talk to Xiaofan, even though she looked like a total counter-revolutionary. He had to smile about this classification, which he still stuck to even though the Cultural Revolution was long gone and even he and Mrs Bo dressed like counter-revolutionaries. Xiaofan was Chinese but spoke English with her partner. But she looked friendly enough, mingling with all the elderly inhabitants of the Xincun.

'Miss,' he said to her one afternoon. 'Could you do an old man a favour?'

'Of course,' she said, walking over with a smile.

'Can you please translate the lyrics of a song? I have this old vinyl but don't understand the meaning.'

He started playing the record. He looked at her ear, as she was concentrating on the music. What a beautiful ear, he thought.

He listened to her voice as she translated the lyrics and was lost. What was the meaning? He realised that all these years he had loved a song whose meaning he did not comprehend, and now that it was translated into Chinese, the meaning was even stranger. It could have been written by someone during the Cultural Revolution, he thought. Someone who was sitting, observing.

We did not learn with every mistake, he thought. He suddenly wished that he could play the guitar and weep. Xiaofan looked at him and he just thanked her. He was too emotional as the time of the Revolution returned to his mind. He played the song again and listened, trying to understand it for the first time in his life.

It was time to have another cigarette.

We made mistakes, he thought, but we were not allowed to be learning, as only the Party defines what a mistake is and what lessons one should learn. But he was the Party, he thought. He, Comrade Bo. People feared him because of his power, even after his prostate had been removed. For years he kept discipline in the area, way beyond the Xincun. He had a job in the district headquarters and not even Mrs Bo knew what he was doing, except that for a while it was public health related. He was the Party. That much was a certainty.

Once he had handed in the keys to his office and emptied the last drawer, he decided this was the end of an era for him. The era that had started when he was 16 and joined the Red Guards. Things were different now. After retirement he fell into a hole as there was nothing left of his old life. He deliberately did not want to hang out with his retired former colleagues, who were meeting in Xujiahui Park to play Mahjong, talk about old times or do early morning Qi Gong exercises in groups to music, with their wives or alone. So he stayed indoors most days, smoking, reflecting about life — with no results. His life was like a broken record, he thought, never moving on. He had to lift the needle and put it into a new row to get going again, but for two years he had been lacking the energy.

One friend he had was Xiaomu. She was the only true member of the Communist Party left. But she was so different from him in her understanding of the role of the Party. He had debated with her, challenging her, as he thought the idea that the Party should serve the people silly. Ludicrous. The Party orders people what to do and people had to be grateful for their decisions — but maybe she had a point. He was not sure anymore after all these years of breathing fear.

But that was the past too. Now he was retired with not much to do. In a way, he envied all the other retirees of the Xincun who were busy with their grandchildren. He had no grandchild to pick up from school, to spoil with ice cream or have a game of table tennis with. Xiaomu had tried to persuade him to make peace with his neighbours, whom she knew he did not get along with. But why should he make the effort? He had tried to become friends with Laowen and Lanfen. He bought Laowen cigarettes and sometimes they smoked together. Laowen listened when he was talking but never said a word. He was strange. How can someone lose the ability to speak. But soon he had to realise that the neighbours did not really want closer contact. If you hear a 'fuck you' when you walk past a window, you get the message. Alas, now he had no power to do anything about it, so he gave up.

One afternoon as he was strolling listlessly about, he came upon a pile of old records in a second-hand shop. Without thinking twice he bought three records. Beatles, Rolling Stones and Pink Floyd.

Again, he asked Xiaofan to help him by translating the text.

She translated the lyrics and added, 'It's difficult. Why are we bricks in walls? Why don't we need education?'

He loved it without knowing why. Such strange lyrics. He offered Xiaofan a cigarette which, to his surprise, she accepted. She inhaled and coughed. He felt very guilty. When he looked at her ear again, he felt a strange arousal even though he knew this was medically impossible.

'In a way, this is what we thought during the Cultural Revolution,' he said. 'We don't need no education.'

She smiled enigmatically at him.

'But did you realise that, all in all, you were just another brick in the wall?' He stared at the wall for a long time in silence without answering. She got up. 'Just one second, I'll be back.'

She returned with two glasses. 'Whisky,' she said. 'Helps you understand English sarcasm. And maybe why we are all just bricks in various walls.'

He did not understand, but the whisky tasted wonderful. It was the first time he had drunk single malt Scotch. It buries sadness, he thought. Xiaofan had a most beautiful face. He studied her fine lines as she sat there listening intently to the next song, 'Shine On You Crazy Diamond'. Her ear was sublime.

'Beautiful music,' she observed. 'No one I know of your age appreciates Pink Floyd or the Beatles, even though the music is from your time. I only discovered Pink Floyd when I started studying at Princeton.' She remained silent for a minute, as her thoughts were drifting away. 'It took a while to understand.'

She finished the cigarette. 'That was disgusting,' she laughed.

Comrade Bo thought that this was the first time in a long while that someone accepted him without prejudice. The neighbours must have told her about him, he figured, and yet she seemed totally open and friendly. Sharing whisky, which was such a treat. Are there people in China without prejudice? Or people who are actually able to forgive? But she had nothing to forgive. And yet, she could have judged him because of his past but she did not, even though she was friendly with all the other neighbours who disliked him.

She translated the lyrics again, and he had to think whether he shone like a sun when he was young.

He did. But it was a dark sun. He closed his eyes and just listened to the song. So this was the music people of his age were listening to in the West, the West he had been instructed to hate. But it was imperialist and colonialist — Marx, Lenin and Chairman Mao were right. And today? He opened his eyes only to see Jing Zhang sitting on the sofa having entered through the door which Xiaofan had left open. He seemed to be listening to the music. Xiaofan looked up.

'Has he got a name?' she asked. 'He always joins us on the terrace even though we rarely have anything for him to eat.

'Jing Zhang. That's what everyone calls him.'

'You mean like the cat in the detective story, Mr Black? Haha, he really looks like it.'

'Yeah, exactly. He is the smartest of the bunch, always observing us through the windows.'

'How old is he?'

'Not quite sure. Maybe fifteen? Maybe older. He appeared one day here at the Xincun. Quite a character. He ignores the other cats, far too aloof to be bothered with riff-raff. But he seems to like your neighbours, particularly Laowen.' He lit another cigarette and continued after observing the smoke for a while.

'And one other neighbour, a cellist, who lives further down the Xincun.'

'Hmm. So cute,' Xiaofan said as Jing Zhang came over and rubbed his fur against her leg.

When the music finished, he put on Pink Floyd again. He liked the last line, he thought, finishing the cigarette.

'You're just another brick in the wall,' he said in English. Xiaofan smiled.

'I guess we all are, but if you pull too many bricks out, the wall collapses, that's what many do not realise.'

He thought about her words and did not understand the meaning, but saw that she smiled innocently and caressed the cat who was purring at her feet.

When the song had ended, she got up and said goodbye. Jing Zhang stretched on the floor and quickly followed her out of the flat. Unsure of what to do, Bo put on the Beatles disc. The music started playing the song, 'While My Guitar Gently Weeps'.

He liked it best. He looked back at the years after his operation and wished he could weep like the guitar. The song ended and he lifted the needle to replay it. And when it ended again, he replayed it again.

Jing Zhang

Jing Zhang was confused as he walked out with Xiaofan. Maybe Comrade Bo had a soul after all?

General Li

General Li had moved into the Xincun only in 2016. Since his retirement he had been living in Guilin as he wanted to be near the Li River and the mountains. There, nobody knew him and he could live in a small house on the outskirts, literally in the middle of a rice field. It was a change from military life. No servants, no one to cook. No one to clean his clothes. No uniform. No salutes. No driver, no car. He had to go out and buy himself clothes and was surprised about the choice. He had taken the deliberate choice to remain anonymous and not to leave any traces of his military past. Finally he had time to study military thinking again. He read Clausewitz again and Brodie, who had developed the concept of nuclear deterrence, ending up each day, however, with Sun Tsu, *The Art of War*, which was brilliant. Written some 2,500 years ago, it was still valid.

Li lived the life of an ascetic, like a monk. He abhorred luxuries and refused to use a car. He had been in the infantry and he was not going to change that. He had walked thousands of miles in his life, like his father who had discovered walking during the Long March. There were only two items of value he possessed. An old Rolex GMT Master and a Leica M3. The Rolex had been a present from a Swiss general he had befriended during an official visit to Switzerland. He had simply taken it off his wrist and given it to him when they bade farewell. The Leica he had bought himself, and it took the most amazing photos. He admired it for the craftsmanship. And for the photos it had produced. He got up to look at the wall where he had hung the five earlier photos he had kept. All black and white. His father and him as a young officer together with Chairman Mao. Another one of him with Deng Xiaoping whom he admired. One together with his Swiss friend when they were hiking in the mountains above Villars. And then two family photos. One of him and his first wife Huafei.

They had been separated, torn apart, during the Cultural Revolution, unable to see each other for almost ten years. When, finally, he was rehabilitated and readmitted to the army, she had moved on. He remembered the long trek to her village in Yunnan in the summer heat. When he had reached her house, he was greeted by another man and their baby. It took Li years to overcome the shock and bitterness. 'Eating bitterness' is what Chinese people call it. He finally understood what that meant as even sweet food tasted bitter. For ten years he had kept himself alive in the hard labour camp by thinking of her and their love. And now there was just emptiness. And the army. He had always kept the picture and still today felt sadness when thinking of her. He still loved her.

The last picture was of his second wife, Biyu, and their son. He was fifty when Fei was born. He did not love Biyu, and soon after the birth he left her when he was sent to another garrison. He tried to love his son, but being in the army made it difficult seeing him in times other than Chinese New Year. Fei only once came to visit him in Guilin.

In his second year in solitude, a dog appeared out of nowhere and decided to settle in Li's garden. Li named him Monty, after Field Marshal Montgomery, whom he admired. He had also named his son after a general, not a British one though. Li loved the dog who seemed as old as him, with grey hair and an air of natural superiority. They would sit for hours in the sunshine and Monty watched Li as he was adding chapters to his book about military strategy. In the summer they went swimming together in the Li River, drifting for miles past the amazing mountains and rice fields. It took them hours to walk home.

When Monty died, Li buried him and went to the temple to burn incenses. He had not been to the temple for decades. The last time he had burned incenses was when his father had died.

In 2014, Li celebrated his 80th birthday. He was content, sitting alone in the morning sunshine, when a car pulled up. Li looked up, recognising the stranger.

Fei. He had not seen him for ages.

Fei had gotten fat. He had written to his father that he worked in Shanghai as an advisor and 'door opener' for foreign banks and private equity companies.

So this is what Fei's grandfather had marched 4,000 miles for.

A woman also got out of the car. Li vaguely remembered her from a photo his son had sent him after their wedding. He had thrown the photo into the bin. She was heavily pregnant and looked at him with sweet eyes.

'I'm Fang.'

Later in the afternoon, as they were walking through the fields, his son finally asked him directly. Fei had been talking for a long time about life in Shanghai, how things had changed, how he, his dad, should not be living all alone in this hut. Li sensed contempt for his asceticism but also expected something else to follow.

'Dad, please move to Shanghai and live with us.'

'Why'

'You can't live here alone. You've become such a hermit.'

'I am very happy here. And you don't even know what I am up to, how I spend my days. You have not even asked about my book.'

'It's all about military strategy, Dad. It does not interest me.'

'I figured.' They walked in silence.

Finally Li said, 'No. It's a no. You have your life and I have mine. I am a communist and you make money out of your status. I do not want to be part of it.'

'But you are. Just by being my father. General Li.'

'What would your grandfather have said?'

They parted and Li sat down in the garden. He missed his father. And Monty.

It took another two years. Li had finished a book about Marshal Zhu De. He was about to walk to the local vegetable shop when a taxi pulled up and Fei's wife Fang got out with a toddler. The toddler ran up to him, clinging on to his leg. Li was again taken by Fang's warm eyes, her smile. His son did not deserve someone as sweet as her. And then the little girl.

'That's Liqin.'

Liqin tried to climb onto his lap. He was slightly taken aback, not used to closeness with people, let alone toddlers. He had hardly ever held Fei in his arms.

At the end of the next afternoon, Fang had persuaded him. They really wanted Liqin to grow up with Ye Ye, Grandpa. And he should not continue living all alone in Guilin. It was not a rational decision. Liqin had persuaded him.

'I will think about it and give you a call.'

'You cannot call us without a phone. Look. We've got you one you can use. It's a simple Huawei.'

He figured using it could not be more difficult than using a machine gun.

'I will call you, please keep it charged.'

Fang hugged him when they departed. Liqin cried, not wanting to leave.

Li had always been a radical general. Taking unexpected decisions had earned him the admiration of his troops and led to rapid promotions. He thought back to his last farewell. He did not want to retire. He had never stayed in a post for long and now he had been living in Guilin for sixteen years. It was time to move on. But he had never before been persuaded by a woman. His Rolex was showing 5 p.m., time for exercises.

Li moved into the Xincun in 2016. In the first two months, he stayed with his son in their apartment on Anting Lu but could not stand the fact that he had no freedom, no life of his own. He did not want to have breakfast, lunch and dinner with them. He did not like their food, it was too rich, too much meat, too western and decadent. He did not drink alcohol. He did not like the fact that the TV was permanently running in the background. The only thing he liked was Fang's smile. She was genuine. And Liqin.

Every morning, he would take Liqin to kindergarten and then pick her up in the afternoon and take her home again. He loved Liqin and Liqin loved him. He tried to understand what had happened to him.

He found a room in the Xincun, sharing a kitchen and bathroom with a cellist and a cat. Perfect.

'I'm Datiqin and that's Jing Zhang.' A detective cat, Li caught himself smiling.

Li loved to listen to the cello music, which sounded so melancholy. He missed Guilin but loved Xuhui, the streets with old trees and the cellist who thought like him. And Liqin who had opened his heart. He was totally surprised by himself.

Liqin

Life had changed when her grandpa appeared. One day he came out of the guest room as Liqin was sitting at the table, watching a video on her tablet. He walked funny, Liqin thought, a bit like the giraffe in the video. And his legs were also skinny like a giraffe's. She liked her dad's belly which she could punch. You could not punch Grandpa without hurting your fist. Her Mom said he looked like a monk. Liqin decided to call him Da Heshang, big monk, a name that stuck and Grandpa did not seem to mind. Da Heshang was a lot more fun than her dad, she thought, as he would play hide and seek endlessly or lift her up to play helicopter. Da Heshang was strong.

With Da Heshang's arrival, Liqin's boring routine stopped. After kindergarten they went to explore town, taking a boat on the Huangpu River, going to the Science Museum among others. One day when she was watching animal videos, Da Heshang got annoyed.

'Stop watching these stupid movies.'

'But I love the animals.'

'There are plenty of cats and dogs in the Xincun.'

'I love Jing Zhang, but these are elephants, zebras, monkeys.'

'Ok. Pack your lunch bag and let's go.'

'Where?'

'Surprise.'

Da Heshang called a cab, and they went all the way out to Shanghai's wild animal park. She could touch an elephant, play with monkeys and have a red parrot sit on her shoulder. Thank sky, thank earth it did not shit on me, she thought when she saw what happened to the boy on whose shoulder the parrot sat next.

'That's a lot of white shit from a red bird,' she observed somewhat shocked.

'Yeah, like politics,' Da Heshang said. Liqin did not understand.

Liqin was proud when Da Heshang picked her up. Her dad had told her that Grandpa had been a big General. She could not quite imagine what that meant, but it sounded important. So if Grandpa was important then she must also be important. Even if Daddy was not. She was thinking how that could work, but found no answer. It was enough that Grandpa was a General, so she would also be one, once she's a grown up.

Being a General seemed to mean doing lots of fun things, like going to the zoo or a boat ride or eating ice cream every day. Daddy never did such things and neither did her friends in kindergarten.

The only dark cloud in Xincun life was Mrs Bo. But Liqin knew she was safe as Da Heshang would protect her. So she could stick her tongue out or pull funny faces which she knew annoyed Mrs Bo. But she needed to drop litter to get her really angry. It worked. But she was nonetheless quite glad that Da Heshang was there to protect her. Mrs Bo never bothered her again, but Liqin was surprised to find her at the post office selling stamps. She decided not to stick her tongue out and just to ignore her.

When Christmas came, Liqin collected four cats with the help of pieces of ham. She put little red hats on each of the cats. Some tolerated the decoration, one ran away. Jing Zhang looked fabulous.

'Must be Buddhist or a Muslim,' Datiqin said, looking after the escaping cat. Liqin did not understand. There were so many things she did not understand, but she thought that once she was a General, she probably would.

Jing Zhang

He was not sure whether at his advanced age he should agree with practical Christianity. He was delighted when General Li moved into the Xincun as it meant that finally Datiqin had a friend. He had been worried about Datiqin who seemed rather lonely. And he loved the little girl, observing how cheeky she was. Once he saw how Liqin threw a paper plane at Mrs Bo from the first floor landing. Sadly, it flew a wide circle around her and Mrs Bo did not notice.

Chen Zaoming

Chen Zaoming moved the knight three paces. He knew that he would beat his friend, even though he wanted to let him win, but Zhong was just too weak a chess player. So even when he deliberately opened himself up for attack, Zhong did not exploit the weak spot. Zhong was a colleague. Though some twenty years younger, Chen liked him most. They had become close friends at Jiaotong University where both worked: Chen as a maths lecturer, and Zhong teaching biology. Chen knew about Zhong's adventures when he was still a student and openly admired him for it.

'Don't you ever regret becoming monogamous?'

'No, no, of course not,' Zhong said. 'The only thing I regret is never having made love to a European girl.' Zhong smiled absentmindedly. Chen looked at him. 'You?' Zhong asked.

'No. Neither. Hmm. But years ago, I fell in love with someone from the States.' Chen's glance focused on the board, not sure which move could most prolong the game. He did not want to win yet as he enjoyed the company of his friend and the soft evening sunlight.

He had been chosen by his department to attend a mathematics congress in Beijing. Early in the morning, he had taken the train from Shanghai. It was the days before fast trains crisscrossed the country and it took him most of the day to reach the capital. He got lost as soon as he left the station since it was already dark. Finally finding a taxi, he reached the hotel. The congress was somewhat unremarkable, but it was the first opportunity for him to meet and mingle with foreigners, which had been frowned upon in the past. Yes, he was teaching modern maths developed by foreigners, but he had not been allowed to travel abroad to meet any other mathematicians, so he was happy when he finally met colleagues from Europe, the States and Japan. Laura was from Boston, and she was the only black academic at the conference. They happened to be sitting at the same table at lunch and were chatting about life in Boston and Shanghai rather than about mathematical problems they were working on, which amused him. A colleague with whom he had studied at Fudan University observed him with suspicion, but Chen ignored him. Jealous jerk, he thought.

In the evening, they went for a stroll to the Yonghe Temple. Many people were burning incense and praying.

'Are people religious?' Laura asked.

'Maybe not religious, but certainly superstitious.'

'I'm a Marxist myself,' Laura said laughing, 'and I certainly do not believe in ghosts, spirits or gods.'

Chen was not so sure himself.

'Tradition,' he said, lighting a bundle of incense sticks.

'For good tradition's sake,' Laura smiled as she also lit an incense stick. 'Maybe my ancestors will now smile down on me.'

They certainly did, Chen thought, when they lay next to each other in bed later that evening. He wondered though, what his ancestors would think if they were able to see him. His grandparents, like most Chinese he knew, were latently racist and the idea of him making love to a black woman gave him additional pleasure.

'Oi,' said Zhong. 'Your move next. Stop dreaming.'

Chen came back to reality.

'You know,' he said, moving a pawn forward. 'Ever since that night, I often have to think about her. Even when I started dating JingJing I could not forget her.'

'Hmm,' Zhong looked at the board. Pawn or knight? He was happily married to Xiaomu and would not dream of making love to other women.

'Do you dream of noodles when your wife has cooked rice?' Chen asked. 'I do.'

'Hmmm, no, actually not.' Zhong answered. 'But that's not the same.'

Chen moved the queen, which was daring.

'Do you think everyone works like that?' Zhong asked. 'I thought only I have these weird thoughts myself.'

Chen moved the queen back.

'I used to think that it's only me, but now I realise most people are like that. Everyone lives both in reality and in fantasy land,' Chen said.

'Yeah. And today's students live in three realities: one in offline life, one online life and one in fantasy land,' Zhong said.

'In the seventies we did not even have fantasy land. Fantasy was just grey smog when you were starving or got beaten up.'

Chen was more macho when talking to Zhong than in reality. Zhong knew that. He knew Chen's wife JingJing, a beautiful and smart woman who worked as a doctor at Xuhui Central Hospital on Huaihai Road. When seeing them, it was very evident they were deeply in love. They sometimes even kissed in public, which is quite taboo. But now that their son was out of the house, they could just do it, they thought. At the Xincun they lived in a small apartment towards the back. Even though it seemed hidden away, Jing Zhang regularly paid them a visit. JingJing thought the cat liked her piano playing.

Their son Donghai was as good-looking as he was stubborn. Barely finishing middle school, he refused to continue doing Gaokao, the finals, and had no interest in a job, playing the guitar instead. Admittedly not badly, but still, in the eyes of Chen and his wife, this was no substitute for university. So he moved out and into the flat of his boyfriend, who was a drummer.

Chen refused to acknowledge that Donghai was gay. Complete cognitive dissonance. Even Zhong knew, and one day Donghai had approached him to ask whether he could talk to his father. When Zhong tried, the chess game was immediately finished. It was a no-go topic, even for close friends.

Chen and JingJing talked about it but he found his wife too resigned to the fact.

'You cannot change him,' she said. But he insisted that with the help of Traditional Chinese Medicine his son could be cured. Secretly, he searched on the internet and in WeChat help groups. He ordered herbal teas. Alas, Donghai refused to drink the stuff.

Chen changed his strategy from herbs to harbouring another hope: if he could find the right girl for Donghai, if he could get Donghai to get laid by a beautiful girl, he would be cured. He never told his wife that he had ordered an escort to Donghai's apartment. The poor girl was chucked out. He cursed himself for having spent a lot of money. He should have taken her when his son refused. Missed opportunity, but strategic planning does not get better with age. Chen was just hoping their friends and neighbours would never find out. What a total disgrace.

So as a next move, from December on, secretly, he joined other parents on Sunday afternoons on People's Square in the middle of Shanghai to look for a partner and advertise his stubborn brat.

The square was full of parents, sitting even in the winter in the cold, with signs stuck to open umbrellas. He read a good many. Anxious parents were posting the qualities of their sons and daughters who they felt were being left behind. In the view of most of the older generation, you were a failure if you were not married with kids by the time you were 30. Or if you were a woman with a PhD.

Finally, when it was already way past 5 p.m., he thought he had found an interesting one: a girl with a

PhD in biology — a failure like his son. Zhong might know her, he hoped. Parents were retired and reasonably good-looking. Father an academic, mother a housewife. Girl with own flat, job, VW Golf. Ideal. Ideal particularly as she, with a PhD, was a no-go for all those men who only have a Masters degree. No man with less than a post-doc would touch a woman with a PhD. Too smart, but Donghai would not mind as he had not even finished high school. Plus she played the sax. Someone so talented must also be good in bed, Chen concluded.

Alas, her parents refused to establish a contact. And Zhong, when asked, had no idea who that biology PhD girl might have been.

Despite his disappointment, Chen tried two other parents but was turned down again. With no higher education, no proper income, no flat of his own and no car to drive, his son was a total loser. Chen did not even dare to put up his own umbrella and decided it might be better to wait till his son had his own concert tour or record label. Then they would all come flying like bees to a honeypot.

Zhong moved the bishop. The situation on the board was totally messed up.

'Guess we won't finish this game today,' Chen said.

'No. Actually I need to get going. Xiaomu will be back soon. Need to buy some rice-wine for dinner first.'

Chen packed up the board and walked back to his apartment and lay down on his bed. Strange to be reminded of Laura today. What had become of her?

They had not stayed in touch, and he never heard from her again after the conference. He waited for a letter but did not write himself. In the end, too much time had passed and he would have felt embarrassed writing to her after a year. She was not at the conference he attended in Xiamen some years later. But that was OK as by then he was in love with JingJing.

He looked at the walls of his study which were covered with calligraphy. Chen was a master of calligraphy, but years ago he had stopped painting bamboo and birds and even writing poetry. He still kept one poem on the wall. He had drawn the characters, black ink on white rice paper, at least a hundred times until he thought it had reached perfection. JingJing thought they all looked the same, but he saw the differences, the tiniest improvements in the stroke of the brush.

When Chen came back from the conference in Xiamen, he decided to paint mathematical formulas. The beauty of the abstract simplicity of numbers, black brush-stroke formulas on a white background, fascinated him. Few people understood this kind of poetry. For some reason, he felt deeply satisfied at this thought.

Jing Zhang

Jing Zhang knew that Donghai was gay. He had no problem with it, as many cats are gay. He had watched him alone in his room cross-dressing and knew where Donghai was hiding his high-heeled shoes. Donghai in stilettos and a tight skirt looked rather cute, particularly when dancing to tech music. Jing Zhang could always recognise gay men, both by the way they walked and by the kindness they had for cats. Gay men were his friends, and Jing Zhang missed Donghai when he moved out of the Xincun.

Donghai

Oh for fuck's sake. Literally. He could not believe it. Throwing himself onto his bed he felt half sick. How could Dad do that to him. It had taken him a huge amount of courage to out himself and then this? Why could Dad not simply accept him? Complete cognitive dissonance. No worse. Denial. Worse. Ignorance. He was furious.

At least his mother tried to understand though she also did not want him to be open about it.

'Your grandparents will have a heart attack.'

So be it. They lived through the war, fought the Kuomintang, survived the Cultural Revolution, why would they be shocked? Well, maybe. Old communists are so totally old-fashioned.

'The neighbours will gossip.'

'Let them.' Donghai could not care less.

But his father? First trying to convert him by giving him some herbal tea to drink that tasted of hetero goat piss and now this?

Then again he felt sorry for the girl. She was very sweet and he admired her Louboutins in which she evidently could not walk. Only his partner could see the humorous side of it.

'Maybe I should have had a go. I used to be bi.'

Donghai did not find it funny at all.

'Dad must have spent a fortune. Did you see the Louboutins?'

'Fake.'

'No. Oh well.' He grabbed his guitar and switched the electricity on. Wham. He loved the sound. Full blast.

The only one who understood him in the Xincun was Xiaomu, with whom he very early on shared his secret and who in the end advised him to move out of his parents' home.

And Jing Zhang, who always seemed to turn up and appear amused when he cross-dressed.

Jing Zhang

All the cats in the Xincun were fervent Maoists. Mao had made China great again and had ensured that their status was restored. Mao, in Mandarin, means cat. Well, with a slightly different intonation, but that's a minor detail. Chairman Mao was definitely a cat lover and Jing Zhang knew it was reported that he lived with at least ten female cats. Jing Zhang, being a natural sceptic, figured that this was a slight exaggeration. But good for him, he thought.

'I bet Obama didn't have ten female cats living in the White House and Trump's wig would not survive one day if he had a single cat.'

'And President Xi?'

'Oh, definitely not.'

So that settled things and explained why the Xincun's maos (cats) were Maoists. Only Maoists, as none of them believed in Marxism. Laowen had read Marx and Engels to Jing Zhang. *Das Kapital*. Jing Zhang had fallen asleep, so boring and irrelevant was that stuff. Total bollocks, he thought, but he was nonetheless wondering what Marx would make of the sharing economy which, in his view, had some communist elements with capitalist characteristics. Cats did not like the sharing economy. Sharing pots and pans and sleeping places was totally unacceptable and so human. Only humans could think of Airbnb, Jing Zhang concluded.

From his position on the various windowsills, Jing Zhang knew that the human sharing economy extended to the love life of some of the Xincun's inhabitants as people sometimes turned up naked, quite unexpectedly it seemed, in other people's apartments. Jing Zhang saw it from time to time from the respective windowsills or from inside the bedrooms. He had found himself some hidden places on the top of wardrobes where he loved to go to after meals to take a nap and had once been woken up by activities on the bed underneath. He was so shocked that he panicked and jumped onto the person's bum, trying to escape. What a sight, he later thought.

From the roofs he climbed, he could also see what was happening inside the apartments on the second floors. The violin teacher who was trying to teach bratlets the art of music, the pianist who regularly fell asleep when her students were playing Chopin. And then also the occasional naked neighbours. He wished he could make a film but operating a camera was beyond his capabilities. He had to realise that amongst his cat friends he was the only one who was interested in the lives of humans. The other cats treated humans with disdain and arrogance.

'Such lack of dignity, elegance and cleanliness,' was the regular complaint.

Unbearably racist, he thought, and no cat seemed to be woke. Too bad.

Xiaomu

Xiaomu carried the bag with Datiquin's vegetables as she was walking next to him. Often, they met at 7 a.m. at the vegetable shop and chatted. Xiaomu was initially surprised by his soft demeanour, thinking that he could have been a Buddhist monk, had he not become a cellist. She instinctively liked Datiqin but also realised that his kindness was not limited to her. He generally treated everyone with politeness and respect. Most people had difficulty understanding his quiet voice, particularly in the vegetable shop where shouting was the norm. She bought leaks and onions and a bag full of eggs, hoping they would not break by the time she had reached the kitchen. At seven in the morning, the air smelled still fresh and mellow and the day had not yet warmed the streets. The sun was visible on the roofs. She also bought a watermelon as she loved the sweet taste. Datiqin seemed frail, she thought, and so it was natural for her to carry his bag back to the Xincun. She was young and felt pretty strong.

'You should join me tonight. There is a concert of the graduating cellists at the Conservatory,' he said.

But Xiaomu was not a great fan of western classical music, preferring Chinese pop.

'Not today, Datiqin,' she said with a warm smile. 'Got to cook dinner for my husband.'

'Oh well. But thanks a lot for carrying my bag.'

She watched him disappear around the corner on the way to his apartment. Xiaomu knew where he lived. And that he had been living in this Xincun all his life.

This week was going to be her big week. In the gallery next to the Xincun, she and Xiofan had organised an exhibition of the lives of the Xincun elders. They had worked closely together and she was pleased that Xiaofan treated her as a friend and equal, even though she had a PhD from an American university and seemed so foreign. At 8 a.m., Xiaomu drank a glass of hot water with herbs. Health was key and herbs helped her fight the heat in her body.

The stereo was blaring out of Comrade Bo's window. Xiaomu thought she knew Bo quite well. Both attended the meetings of the Communist Party, where he was the elder but she was chairing the meetings. People generally disliked him, even now that he was retired. And yet there was a side to him that she thought was fascinating. She heard Bo singing along. 'We had riots in the classroom.' This really sounded like the Cultural Revolution, she thought. Her own parents and grandparents had never ever spoken about those years, but she had heard a lot about it from the other elderly inhabitants of the Xincun. She knew that Comrade Bo had played, shall we say, a more active role than strictly necessary. This was not the image of the Party she wanted to portray. To Xiaomu, the Party had to serve the people, and the people were her people in the Xincun. And she was the Party. She was more than happy that Mrs Bo had been asked to go by her own boss. Mrs Bo was destructive to the neighbourly spirit and community Xiaomu tried to build.

She knocked on Bo's door. It was going to be a difficult conversation, but she hoped he would co-operate.

Bo listened carefully till she had finished and in the end he sighed. 'I had not intended to participate,' he said. 'I'd hate to have my story and my photos plastered on the wall. Besides, you know, most people have an issue with me here.'

'That's why you have to make an effort, Comrade. You can't be stuck in the past forever.'

'Haha, that's exactly what Xiaofan told me too,' he replied. He got up and put on a record. 'Ask General Li.' Putting down the needle, he looked at her from the side.

'My favourite. I picked it up during those days and only realised what the music meant when Xiaofan translated the lyrics. And now I often feel like weeping like the guitar.' He paused and with difficulty got up again. Looking out of the window he said, 'You know, I will participate if you play this song in the gallery.'

'Deal,' Xiaomu said with a smile. Bo looked surprised.

'I thought you would decline.'

On her way back to the office, she saw Jing Zhang stretching on a windowsill, soaking up the sunshine. She liked the cats in the Xincun and Jing Zhang was her favourite. She liked stroking his black fur and his purring. She felt equally responsible for the cats as for the humans. In her Xincun, everyone seemed equal. Also the kids. Respect for the elderly was the basis of Chinese society, derived from Confucius, whom she had studied at length. But she wanted to have the same respect also for children as she came to realise that children have their own kind of wisdom.

She had quarreled with Mrs Bo about this.

Xiaomu kicked the ball back to the little boy who was kicking it against the wall where he was hitting an imaginary soccer goal. He passed it back to her. She was quite good at sports and lobbed the ball over his head right into the goal.

'Goal, goal,' he cried.

Having also talked to General Li, she now had everyone who mattered. She had to discuss this with Xiaofan. This would be an amazing exhibition about decades of life in their Xincun. She would invite the Party leaders from the district and was secretly hoping that they would bring the big wigs along, if they liked it. It would be good for her career. Having General Li's story meant every Party leader would have to pay a visit out of respect. They would like it as Xiaofan knew her stuff. She watched as the stories unfolded on the walls. Amazing photos, but she had received instructions not to stress the time of the Cultural Revolution too much. It was part of history, she thought. So why not? If we want to be modern, we have to learn from history. Her husband agreed. Sadly, also many Chinese

Communists were quite bolshy and even her boss could not change their narrow-minded opinions.

As she walked up the staircase to Xiaofan's terrace, she envied her. What a beautiful place, quiet and secluded. But it was not the apartment or the terrace, nor the fact that this now had become Jing Zhang's favourite hangout place. The thing that really astonished Xiaomu was the ease with which Xiaofan had become friends with all the elderly people in the Xincun. Everyone knew her and had told her their stories, including private details of their childhoods, the hard years in the 1960s and early 1970s, and the challenges of dealing with the present which were different but for many a lot easier to deal with than the past.

'Alone?' she asked Xiaofan when she had reached the terrace. She had expected her to be with her partner.

'He flew off to Amsterdam for some board meeting, I think.'

Xiaomu was slightly taken aback by how unconcerned Xiaofan was.

'Oh, he travels once a month to Europe, so if I were worried about his plane crashing, I wouldn't be able to sleep at all. But, tell me, have you managed to persuade Comrade Bo?'

It was clear he was somehow central to the exhibition and yet she thought only people with intimate knowledge of the Xincun would understand the subtleties that the mix of the lives on one wall would display.

It was evening when she closed the door to her office. She smiled at the photos of President Xi and Chairman Mao. She liked the sincerity of Xi. And Mao was the immortal and would remain the only immortal, she thought. Well, maybe Deng too. She had decided to put up a photo of Deng Xiaoping as well, above her desk. She had found one a few years ago of Deng practicing calligraphy, his eyes focused on the brush. Black and white.

She walked back to Xiaofan's terrace to tell her that she had to cut stuff out about the Cultural Revolution, but the terrace was empty. She sat down in the armchair and savoured the silence around her. This was Shanghai, her Shanghai: quiet, birds, bees and in the distance the Beatles out of Comrade Bo's apartment. Was it her role to bring reconciliation to the people of her Xincun? What would it take? No one would publicly ask for forgiveness and no one would publicly forgive. Many years ago, she remembered seeing a photo in an article about how the former German Chancellor, Willy Brandt, knelt down in Warsaw. A gesture asking for forgiveness of crimes he had not committed but which his country had committed during the war. It was immensely powerful, she thought. And yet some of her friends did not agree, thinking Brandt lost face by kneeling down. What would Confucius have said to that gesture? She was sure he would have agreed that great strength derives from humility. She thought about the state of the Party and realised that humility was not part of the current five-year plan.

But General Li was humility personified. Well, mixed with a bit of aloofness. She felt that aloofness was justified. And yet she admired him for how he dealt with his granddaughter, cheeky Liqin. He was different from other grandparents as he managed to speak her language and be with her as if there was no age distance, no difference. Equally, Liqin seemed different from the other kids as she was smart, witty and cheeky. She noticed how Liqin disliked Mrs Bo.

Jing Zhang decided to jump onto her lap, waking her out of her thoughts. Still no sign of Xiaofan, but she could smell Laowen smoking on the half-landing beneath her. When he had retreated back to the kitchen, she left the terrace. It was time to cook dinner.

Zhong

Zhong looked into the microscope and saw the cells moving under the glass in slow motion. What a random way of moving about. He smiled as the thought occurred to him that this is like life in politics. Everywhere.

The alarm on his smartphone indicated it was noon, waking him out of his contemplations. The students stormed out of the lab. Peace again.

Studying biology has been a pretty safe subject, as his father had told him when he was 18. He did not want to join the Party and had no political ambitions. Whether there is democracy or what he called a Communist theocracy did not matter to him. It was quite funny, he thought, that he married a Communist official, in a way like instant Karma for his heresy. But he loved her and if every Communist were like Xiaomu, the world would definitely be a better place and more countries would be communist. Alas Xiaomu's Communism only existed in her Xincun. That's why he loved her.

Zhong had a few girlfriends while he was a student. Whilst initially he was competing with his male fellow students to see who would be able to get the most beautiful one, he soon realised they were no competition. He also noticed he was restless and could not stay for long with one. But nonetheless it was him who generally got dumped. By the time the second Chinese New Year at university arrived, he concluded enough is enough.

He took the train to visit his parents. His father had been a teacher in a secondary school who had decided not to return to teaching after the Cultural Revolution. He was too traumatised, having been beaten up and publicly shamed by the kids he thought he had dedicated his life to.

'Let those little fuckwits just die in ignorance,' he said when things were finally over in 1976. He became a librarian instead, collecting, hording and guarding knowledge. Zhong remembered his father sitting behind a desk in the library, eyeing visitors with suspicion. 'Make libraries out of cowsheds,' was his motto. Only many years later did Zhong understand, when he read the harrowing story of the Peking University professor Ji Xianlin, *The Cowshed*. Ji had spent the years of the Cultural Revolution imprisoned and tortured. All the cells where people got imprisoned were referred to as cowsheds.

'Burning books could become fashionable again before you know it,' he told his son. 'But this time I'm prepared.' He smiled at Zhong. 'You should always learn from your mistakes.'

As if the times when books got burned would return anytime soon. Zhong was not sure about it as he thought about his fellow students, not only the ones whom he met in bed. None of them were particularly revolutionary. All of them wanted to progress in life, study, complete a PhD or post-doc abroad, ideally at a US university or, failing that, in the UK. But many colleges there, he was told, were so swamped with Chinese that they might just as well teach in Mandarin. So why go there if you only meet Chinese? Isn't the fun of being abroad that you can meet as many nationalities as possible? And then his students wanted jobs. Well-paid jobs, not lowly paid ones at uni. And not only in labs or working for pharmaceutical companies. It was quite eye-opening for him to see how many ended up in finance or with McKinsey. They were all so capitalist. He had to smile, thinking about his father who would have loved this generation. Yes, some were nationalistic, but the idea of marauding around campus burning books and beating up lecturers? With their Louis Vuitton bags? Laughable. What had come over those idiots in 1966? He had no answer but felt sure that history would never ever repeat itself, even if, as his father would quote Mark Twain, it would rhyme. His father was more pessimistic.

It was his father who had advised him to study biology and to work in a lab, away from people. People cannot be trusted, he used to say.

'Just trust whatever you see under your microscope.'

Zhong knew he could not talk to his parents about girls, as their zen-like existence made him realise the futility of his pursuits of the most beautiful female students. So he thought. He was sure his parents had been living like celibate monks ever since he had been conceived as he had only experienced them as living in Buddhist celibacy, distant and in parallel worlds. He never, ever saw them kiss or even hug.

When he got back, he made love to his two last girlfriends and then gave up. Till exams, he decided. I could be a monk, he thought after the first month of celibacy. This celibacy lasted and he seemed to enjoy the freedom.

In his last year at university, he met Xiaomu and immediately fell in love. Whilst he was preparing for the finals, they got married. He never again wanted to make love with anyone but his wife and looked back at his early student days in disbelief and felt morally superior to his previous self. And to Chen, though he did not show it as he liked him too much.

Xiaomu and he had a very small flat in the Xincun and they decorated it the way they thought modern intellectuals would decorate it. Ikea style. He was in awe when he made his first trip to the huge shop on Caoxi Road and amused to see so many people sleeping in the showroom beds. Maybe he should also take a nap to try out the beds before buying one. Later, when he sat back in the comfortable Swedish armchair and looked at his books, he saw how Xiaomu smiled.

'I always wanted to travel to Scandinavia to see the beauty of the North, but now I think we don't need to anymore. We have it here.'

'Glad we did not buy any Italian furniture, then,' Zhong answered laughing. 'I still want to visit Rome with you.'

Just when he had finished slowly undressing Xiaomu and started kissing her white skin, Jing Zhang appeared on their windowsill.

'Look, here he is again. Little voyeur.'

'He looks so sad ever since he got castrated. Let's close the curtains so that he does not need to see what he is missing.' Xiaomu got up and Zhong looked at her slender naked body. She moves about like a cat, he thought, as she slowly closed the curtains. His last glance was at Jing Zhang's disappointed face.

Jing Zhang was Zhong's favourite cat and, usually, when he appeared on the windowsill, he would open the window to let him in. Jing Zhang then normally disappeared to lie on top of the books on the top bookshelf, where Zhong kept a collection of novels. Funny how he seemed to be so intellectual. When he was working on his laptop, the cat would frequently come to sit beside him and watch him type. Almost as if reading what Zhong was typing.

Zhong spent hours working on papers he needed to publish to stay in the academic rat race. He sometimes hated it and thought about the quiet and satisfying life of his parents. Would he like to guard a library? It sounded like an ideal job for him, sitting behind a desk, reading incoming books, ideally comics, making sure that children did not misbehave.

But then again, he was tempted by big pharma. Recently, a head-hunter had contacted him as the Chengdu Institute of Biological Research was beefing up its vaccine capacity. They had had a major breakthrough supplying vaccines against Japanese encephalitis to UNICEF and were seeking to develop more vaccines.

'Don't trust big business,' his father had warned him. 'They will just exploit you.'

But Chen was more encouraging.

'Think of the money in addition to the mission. You'd be earning easily ten times what you are making today, and then you can also jump ship and work for Pfizer in the States.' Chen still seemed to be dreaming about the States. 'Think of the women …'

Zhong gave him a blank stare.

'Oh well,' Chen concluded.

Zhong was not sure. At heart, he was a nerd who loved his life at uni, his students, and what would Xiaomu do in the States, where not many head-hunters were looking for experienced Communist Party officials?

When he declined, Xiaomu hugged him.

'Let's rather travel to Italy together. And for now, how about pizza at Green and Safe?'

His favourite restaurant on Dongping Road. He opened the window and Jing Zhang jumped in, had a look around and jumped out again. He still does not know how to walk without balls, Zhong thought, watching how Jing Zhang disappeared down the lane.

Datiqin

Datiqin kept his eyes closed when the last note had totally dissolved in the ensuing silence. This silence was the essence, he thought, the essence of Bach. And Bach was Dasein. Pure Dasein. He loved the Sarabande and could not comprehend how someone could compose such abstract music back in the 1720s. Ethereal, like Rothko's paintings or like his love for Ming used to be. Whenever the last note of the Sarabande faded away, he was reminded of her, her fine smile, her hands, her pale lips.

When he finally opened his eyes, Jing Zhang was sitting on the couch, observing him. He usually arrived shortly after the Prelude and listened patiently. What an unusual cat, he had thought when Jing Zhang first arrived at his door. He had meowed outside whilst he was playing the cello inside. When finally Datiqin had opened the door, Jing Zhang slowly walked into the room and sat down in the armchair, waiting for the music to continue. He never came for food, which was strange, but Datiqin gathered that he was fed elsewhere and only came to listen to the music. Over the years he observed that Jing Zhang's favourite composer was Bach. And of all the suites, he liked the Sarabande of the fifth suite best. Like Ming, Datiqin reflected as he realised how his throat was tightening. Even after all these years, he often felt tears running down his face when he had finished playing the Sarabande. He savoured the taste of salt. Sadness always overcame him, and sometimes he played it twice. Abstract, an expression of absolute perfection, light, sad, and, yes, ethereal. Like his love for Ming.

Jing Zhang had not moved a millimetre, observing him as he put down his bow, as if waiting for something. But the only thing that could manifest itself from this music was snow. White snow, covering sadness, music, love, the past. He picked up his bow again and continued playing till he had finished the whole suite and Jing Zhang got up and went to the door, which Datiqin opened for him. As if saying thank you, Jing Zhang turned around and looked at Datiqin before disappearing down the staircase.

Datiqin never got his job at the Conservatory back. With only three fingers to use, he was not able to play the whole repertoire that he knew so well how to teach. He figured that playing Schumann's or Dvorak's concertos, Boccherini or the last Bach suites would never sound the same again. For some movements of the first suites, you would not notice a difference whether one played it with four fingers or he with three. When you play the higher notes using the thumb, no one uses the little finger in any event. When he was asked to audition after the Cultural Revolution to get his old job back he had not been ready. He had not played the cello for ten years and was rusty. As rusty as all the others, who all had four fingers plus the thumb to play with. They turned him down. They. Some were his former colleagues.

He asked about Ming, but people did not know where she was.

He felt totally empty and without hope and wandered aimlessly all around town till he reached the Huangpu River after midnight. He had stood for a long time on the bridge, unsure whether he should end his life. What was life without music? It was snowing, which was unusual for Shanghai, and soon he was totally covered in snow. He was wearing no gloves and the little finger of his left hand hung listless and cold. He could barely move it. Datiqin started crying, listening to his inner sounds where he could hear Schumann's concerto, the music he was judged too rusty to play, the music he would never again play like Pablo Casals.

In 1962, barely 21, his professor feted him as the young Casals. In fact, he had given his first concert when he was still at middle school. Boccherini. In his twenties, he played Dvorak, Elgar. Schumann's concerto became his favourite. He taught at the Conservatory till the day they came and destroyed the place.

Most of his memories are gone. But he still remembered getting a plaster around his left hand from a nurse and feeling his hair wet with blood. Somehow he had made it home. For ten years he was lucky to have a job as a janitor at Zhongshan hospital. At least he was allowed to stay in Shanghai and did not have to go to work in the countryside, which would have killed him.

But then again, this would have probably been the better outcome, freezing to death in a field in Xinjiang Province, he thought whilst looking from the bridge at the black water of the Huangpu River. He watched how the snowflakes drifted by endlessly, disappearing into the black abyss where the river was. He tried to listen to any noise but realised there was only silence except for the wind and the snowflakes drifting by. It was hypnotising, he reflected, as he was getting colder and colder, unable to decide whether to jump or, rather, when to jump. Gradually his mind turned blank and black, like the abyss beneath him.

Jump.

Out of nowhere a hand touched his shoulder.

'Don't. Otherwise, they would have got what they wanted,' a deep male voice hidden underneath a hat and a huge winter coat said, gently but firmly pulling him away from the railing. The stranger put his arm around his shoulder and slowly started walking, pushing Datiqin along with quiet determination. Through the heavy snow, Datiqin could see the dim lights of the Bund. As if in a trance, he gradually progressed forward, pushed by the stranger. After they had walked for a while, and the stranger thought they were safe, he stopped and got out a small bottle. He opened it and handed it to Datiqin. Datiqin took a long sip and swallowed the biting yet mellow liquor, feeling the soothing warmth in his stomach. His inner paralysis slowly faded. The stranger looked at him from underneath his hat. It was dark and Datiqin could not really see his face, even when it was lit for brief moments by the distant lights. They continued walking in silence next to one another. Now without being pushed by the stranger, Datiqin felt able to walk alone. At the end of the bridge, the stranger urged him to finish the bottle. Again, Datiqin felt the warmth inside, mingled with gratitude. The stranger put his arm around his shoulder and then turned around and walked away. Within a minute he had disappeared in the darkness. Datiqin was alone again, but the river was now behind him and he had no intention of going back.

His cello had been destroyed. He could not save it from the brutality of the Revolutionary Guards. It was built in 1776 in France and had survived so many wars and even the Japanese occupation. Were the Japanese more civilised than the Revolutionaries? That it was built in pre-capitalist days did not impress the Red Guard who broke it with one kick into the cello's stomach. Sometimes Datiqin could still hear the cracking of the wood and the noise of the string that snapped.

After the Revolution, when he thought things were safe again, he went to visit his parents. In the attic he found his first cello. It had survived these years. The strings were somewhat loose; but he could tune it, and it stayed tuned. The bow was in perfect condition. He found a small block of rosin and put it onto the hair of the bow. Datiqin had absolute pitch and did not need a tuning fork like many of his colleagues. A. D. G. C. Four strings, four distinct sounds. The cello's sound had not changed much, he realised, even after all those years of not having been played. He was overcome by immense gratitude.

It was not a great instrument but good enough for him now that he did not have to play for anyone but himself. His throat tightened when he played it, and he remembered the sounds of playing it as a child. Memories from his childhood came back. His mother who had pushed him to practise. His father, who was only interested in his own research. The difficulty playing the sixth suite. He tried to play it again but failed, gradually realising that it might forever be too difficult to play without his little finger. Depressed, he took the cello and bade farewell. His mother smiled a sad and melancholy smile.

The following day he was back at Zhongshan hospital, cleaning the floors and toilets. He knew there were only two possibilities. Either jump from the bridge or become a cellist again. The former was no longer a possibility. In the evening, he got out his cello and started practising. Scales. Etudes. More scales. He stretched his third finger to play the notes his fourth should have played. Only after fourteen days did he try Bach's Cello Suite No. 1. Already after the first few notes, he needed his little finger. He stretched his third finger and it did not work as he wanted it to work. Depressed, he walked out of the house. No wonder they had turned him down. He should have practiced for a year before applying. But then again, he also knew that deep inside he did not want to rejoin the Conservatory. The place was haunted with too many memories. Ming. Ma. The sound of the foot crushing his cello, ending its beautiful life that had started in 1776.

Near the gate he bumped into Laowen. They decided to take a walk together. Laowen finally dared to ask Datiqin about his finger. He looked at it for a long time and shook his head. In silence they walked down the street for a while.

'I got beaten up so many times, but thank God they did not break any bones,' Laowen said.

'Lucky you.'

'Yeah, that's what I thought. And I spoke German, so I was suspicious.'

'How did they find out?'

'My books.'

'I thought you hid them.'

'I did. But they found those I could not squeeze under the floorboards. With hindsight, it was quite funny that they even burnt *Das Kapital*. Uneducated idiots.'

Datiqin knew that Laowen was an engineer who produced the most beautiful pens, but did not understand why one needed to speak German to engineer pens. He did not speak any German and still could play Bach.

'Would I experience Bach differently if I spoke German, Laowen?' he asked.

'Don't know.' Laowen looked thoughtful. 'As an engineer, I appreciated the precision and accuracy of German language and, it may sound strange, but it made me feel as if I could even perfect fountain pens once I understood German.'

'So are you suggesting I should have studied music in Germany to understand Bach better?'

Laowen smiled enigmatically.

After a month, Datiqin could play the first Bach suite reasonably well again. He had to retrain, playing everything without his little finger which was difficult as intuitively he still wanted to use it. His memory had come back, and he could once again play everything by heart. His fingers remembered what to do, except that he had to retrain them to remember and play differently. He opened the music of the fifth suite and turned to the Sarabande. Slowly he started playing. But it was too much. Emotions overcame him. Ming. Where was she? Why could he not find her? He put the cello aside and looked at his hands, his fingers which were hard and damaged from cleaning hospital toilets. He went towards the gates of the Xincun to have a walk and on his way saw Comrade Bo.

He knew everyone hated Bo and that he had all the reasons to hate him too. His finger. His work as a janitor. And yet, he could not feel any hatred, just sadness and pity. Bo would suffer badly in his afterlife for all the crimes he had committed on earth. It was not for us humans to judge and take revenge, he thought. Datiqin smiled at Bo when their eyes met but Bo's face remained expressionless. Maybe that is my way of punishing him, by reminding him of who he was and what he had done. The past is like a big black cloud and Datiqin was sure it was haunting Bo at night. He had forgiven Bo long ago.

Six months after he had taken up practicing the cello after work, one evening someone knocked at his door. It was a neighbour whom he vaguely recognized. She wanted to find a teacher to teach her daughter to play the cello. She had heard him practice every evening when she came home from work and said that she often listened to him underneath his window. The music moved her and she thought it would make her daughter a better person.

By the end of the year, he had quit his job as a janitor to concentrate on teaching the cello.

After two years, he stopped going to the Conservatory to ask for Ming. He realised she might never return. He had searched all the other music colleges and music schools but there was no trace of her.

When he learned that Ma had died during the Revolution, a deep sadness engulfed him. Ma, his soulmate, teacher and competitor. She had been the most amazing cellist and a young and humble teacher. He had loved the way she played Elgar's cello concerto. It was as if the cello played her. Ma used to fall into a trance when she played. She did not need to look at the conductor or the orchestra to communicate. She had become the music. And now, Ma was dead. Suicide. Datiqin knew she would not have committed suicide, even if all her fingers were broken, even if they had destroyed her ears so that she could no longer hear. He remembered Ma joking about losing her hearing when they were sitting eating hot-pot together with Ming.

'Look, Beethoven couldn't hear a thing when he composed his Nineth Symphony. When I'm too old, deaf and arthritic to play the cello, I'll compose. And if I can't write anymore, I'll just sit and savour the music inside my head. I do not need to hear it to enjoy it. I have the most comprehensive music library inside my head.'

They murdered you, he thought when he stood at Jing An temple burning incense for Ma. But they will not kill your spirit.

Five years after the end of the Cultural Revolution, Datiqin's life had normalised. He had a large number of students of all ages who came to his flat for lessons. His life had become a routine, but he avoided going to the Conservatory.

One evening he saw a woman walking through the Xincun gates. Ming, he thought. He was too far away to recognise her, and she disappeared too quickly between the houses. The guard did not know where she lived. Two months passed till he saw the figure again. He knew it was her, the way she walked. She had gotten a lot thinner, but her back was straight and her stride was fast. Faster than his. He could not catch up with her but managed to see her disappear into one of the houses at the end of the Xincun.

The next evening he knocked at her door, unsure how she would react. Too much time had passed, he thought. And Ma was gone. Ma, whom they both had loved.

The second time they met, Ming held him close as if afraid to let him go. He could feel her heart beating underneath the thin shirt as they stood by the window. Making love to Ming was impossible — too ethereal felt her body. He touched her hair and looked into her deep and melancholy eyes.

Walking back to his room in the total darkness and sensing the cold morning air, a feeling of immense gratitude overtook him. He would love Ming forever, platonically, the same way he loved music.

As Jing Zhang scratched at the door, begging to be let in, he was taken out of his thoughts back to reality. Jing Zhang stretched out on the table, waiting to be stroked. Thirty years had passed since Ming had died, and yet he felt even today great sadness thinking of her. He was wondering what she would have thought of today's China, having experienced the last years of the war as a teenager, the years since 1949 and then since 1976. What would she have made of the amazing changes since the beginning of the new millennium?

He did not know anymore himself what to make of it. On the one hand, he loved the new Shanghai, the concerts, the shops, the little restaurants. Even he could afford to have lunch or dinner at H2, the restaurants on Jianguo Road or at Green and Safe. Unimaginable forty years ago. The quality of the Conservatory was world class. What a contrast to 1979, when there was not a single tuned grand piano in the whole of Shanghai when Isaac Stern visited.

But since General Li moved into his building and they chatted in the kitchen in the mornings, his view had become more nuanced. Had China become a mix of billionaires and materialism? General Li practised what he preached: asceticism. Was it generational? Even Li's son did not follow his father's example.

But Li's granddaughter Liqin was taking after her Grandpa. So maybe there was hope for China.

Someone knocked at his door. He opened it. The new tenant living above Laowen's place stood at the door.

'Come on in,' Datiqin said.

'I wanted to ask you whether I can have some cello lessons.'

'I don't teach beginners.'

'Well, I can play Bach Suites Nos.1-3 but what I really want to learn is to play the Sarabande of the fifth suite.'

'Why?'

'Because I sometimes hear you play it and it sounds just so intense and yet abstract.'

'Hmm…,' said Datiqin as he walked over to Jing Zhang to caress his ears. He felt he could not teach it. It reminded him too much of Ma.

Ming

Ming was fifty when she moved into the Xincun. Before the Cultural Revolution she had been Datiqin's colleague at the Conservatory, where she taught the piano. She never spoke of the years in exile, not even to Datiqin when they met again in 1981.

Ming was walking back to her room in the small apartment she shared with two other families. The place had been unbearably filthy. It took her days to clean her room once she had moved in so that it became habitable. A former colleague gave her a piano as a present. Or was it as compensation for what had happened to her? She hung up a picture of calligraphy which her father had given to her and which had survived the Cultural Revolution. Magically. She liked to have things black and white. Or grey, concrete grey, like her walls. The only signs of colour were the two red stamps on the calligraphy and the one flower she always kept on the black piano. She only dressed in black, grey and white.

Initially, Ming did not want to go back to teach at the Conservatory as she thought she had finished with that part of her life. She could not bear the idea of teaching again in the institution that had been trampled upon and that had trampled upon her. She was happy doing office work. But then her former colleagues came and pleaded with her to return. But could she go back to a place which was so full of memories? She thought about her former colleagues who were now back, bringing the Conservatory back to life. They had all had awful experiences and yet they returned.

'It is for the music and for the next generation of students,' the Head of the Conservatory told her. 'We could not continue but I knew they would not be able to destroy our spirit and our dignity. Our dignity derives from the music.' Ming asked for a cigarette and opened the window.

'How can you talk about dignity when they killed Ma?' she asked.

'The only way you can deal with her death is by defying them, and you can only defy them when you do what you and Ma used to love doing. Playing music. Teaching music. Making sure that music lives everywhere. Making sure Ma continues living through your music rather than dying a second death through your silence.'

'My fingers are rusty.'

'Practise.'

Ming left without an answer and went to the Jing An temple to pray. Now that Ma was dead, Ming felt that she needed prayers to communicate. But how many times had she prayed, and how many times had she wondered why her prayers were not answered? She had felt like turning atheist — but then again, her Buddhist belief gave her strength. Ming reflected upon the concept of dignity and knew that it was dignity even more than religion that had kept her alive. They had tried to crush her dignity as she was a class enemy. Her father had been a wealthy capitalist roader. She had studied music in Paris and London. Chopin was her favourite composer. But they had not succeeded. As a Buddhist she feared she would have given up, hoping to continue in her next incarnation. She stuck to dignity.

She sat down and opened the piano and started playing. Mazurka Opus 63. It was the music that had stayed in her ears when she was interrogated and it was the music that gave her both sadness and self. She had left each interrogation with her head high. They did not dare hit her. But why did Ma have to die? She knew she would never be able to find an answer. And there would be no justice.

She told the Director she would rejoin.

Coming back from teaching one evening, she could hear cello music from one house in the Xincun. She turned left to follow the sound and saw the open window. Saint-Saëns, 'The Swan.' She wanted to cry but her eyes were dry. She felt her throat tightening.

Ma.

The piece that had melted them together. She remembered playing it with her and how their souls felt like one.

A neighbour walked past and she could not move, standing underneath the window as if paralysed. How many times had she accompanied Ma as she played this piece. Abstract music, sublime and beautiful. She thought it had been destroyed during the Cultural Revolution, yet here it was again, in the air. It had been more than music to both of them — a deep expression of purest love.

Ma. A woman her age, from Hainan, incredibly talented. Ming had learned that Ma had jumped from the building. Total lies, she thought, knowing that Ma would never jump. Now pictures of their days playing music together at the Conservatory flooded her mind like heavy rain. They had been more than soulmates. It was an incredible closeness, an understanding without the need to talk, communication through music by playing Beethoven or Chopin Sonatas, the Sonata No. 65 in G Minor. Or 'Le Cygne, The Swan', their favourite. Ming felt that sometimes they were like birds who can fly totally synchronised without communicating, or, rather, communicating without words, instant knowledge and awareness of what the other does, thinks, feels, desires. She loved Ma's dark eyes, full of laughter, her freckles, her soft skin which was slightly tanned, so unusual for a Chinese woman. She could, even now, feel her touch, those incredibly delicate and long fingers on her skin.

The music stopped, waking her out of her dream. Ming waited for a moment to see whether it would continue, but then decided to go back to her room.

At home she cooked a simple dinner. Rice and pak choi. She did not eat meat, believing that man has no right to kill other creatures. After dinner she lay down on her hard mattress. There were three luxuries she allowed herself in life. Music, love and cigarettes. She lit one, thinking about the other two. Music she had managed to rediscover after twelve years of emptiness. She could still play Chopin but she would never be able to play Saint-Saëns again. And love?

She inhaled and enjoyed the feeling as the smoke filled her lungs. Slowly, she blew the smoke into the room where it drifted towards the window and out into freedom. Elusive, she thought, looking at the smoke, like thoughts in the wind. Like love.

Again, she had to think of Ma. Ma was always on her mind, even years after they last saw each other. Like so many evenings before, they had been playing music together at the Conservatory and then Ma had set off to meet with her uncle. The next day, the Revolutionaries had ransacked the place and she had been arrested. That was the last time. Ming felt sadness for a long time never to have said a proper goodbye to Ma, and it was only after the Revolution that she was told that Ma had died. It was the end of the world for Ming, the end of being, it took away the essence of life, it destroyed the music inside her. Ming could not touch a piano for years but then realised it would not help anyone if she stopped playing altogether and it would not bring Ma back.

Months passed and she sometimes heard cello music coming from that window, but never again 'The Swan'. It sounded as if someone was teaching, as most of the time the music was pretty atrocious. She decided not to pass the window anymore and walked another way from the gate to her room.

She was back as a professor and loved teaching eager students who played with technical brilliance and passion. Teaching was exhausting though. The Director had told her she needed to take care of herself.

Ming looked down at her naked body as she washed herself, remembering his words. The water was lukewarm at best. She had always been skinny, but now she was just skin and bones. Few muscles. No fat. She touched her breasts, they were non-existent. She was wondering whether she had vanished as a woman whilst remaining alive as a musician. After Ma, she had never had similar feelings for anybody else. After Ma, there could no longer be this kind of love. Carefully, she dried herself. She looked at her feet, her skinny toes. Her feet were delicate, as were Ma's. She remembered looking at Ma's left foot when they were playing together, how it accompanied the music, almost like a drummer, delicate, beautiful and precise.

She dried herself and put on a clean, dark grey shirt and went back to her room and decided to go straight to bed.

Ming hardly ever read novels, preferring to read either some music scores or a book about a musician. At the Conservatory, she had borrowed the biography of Pablo Casals. She would be able to dream about the music whilst reading it, dream of playing it, accompanying the cello part. Should she write a book about Ma? Her short or shortened life?

Suddenly, there was a knocking at her door. She first wanted to ignore it, but the knocking was persistent.

'Come in,' she finally shouted, sitting up in bed. A gentleman opened the door.

'Ming?' He paused in the doorway. 'May I come in?' the man said.

She did not know what to say, trying to figure out where she might know the voice from. He took a step forward till the light shone on his face. To her utter amazement, she recognised Datiqin, who had aged. She remembered him as a young student, then as a colleague, a competitor for the attention of Ma.

'Datiqin,' she said with a broad smile. 'Unbelievable. You. Here.'

He closed the door behind him, and they embraced for a long time. She felt his bony shoulders as he felt hers and both recognised how they had aged. Less material, less body and more soul, she thought.

She analysed his left hand, the broken finger that prevented Datiqin from being there in the same league as her friend the cellist Jian Wang, and yet she sensed no bitterness in his words or in his smile.

He shares the luxuries in my life, Ming later thought. Cigarettes and music and platonic love.

She realised she loved Datiqin and felt love in his smile, his words and, above all, in the way he played the cello for her. Datiqin continued loving her the way she wanted to be loved. Abstract. Platonic. It helped her overcome Ma's death, she thought. Ma had been the only one she could physically love and after her death all desire for physical love had died too, Ming realized.

She wondered how Ma would feel about her platonic love for Datiqin and asked her the next time she prayed at Jing An temple. It started raining and Ming continued burning incense, waiting for an answer from Ma which never came. She was totally soaked by the time she arrived back home.

And yet, she did not want to play together with Datiqin, preferring to hear him play Bach. Endlessly. She also loved to have him sit and listen as she played Chopin. When one day he started playing 'The Swan,' she asked him to stop.

In the late spring of 1989, Ming got bronchitis. Her body was weakened from night-long discussions about democracy and freedom at her home and at the Conservatory. She had wanted to join the students on Tiananmen Square but in the end, she decided to stay in Shanghai and teach.

Datiqin took her to hospital when her condition worsened and she started coughing blood. She lived on, getting weaker and weaker as the antibiotics started kicking in. Her face was all white when Datiqin visited her on the day that was to be her last day. She smiled at him when his face appeared above the bed and then smiled again, as he disappeared as if into a big white mist.

'Now I will be with Ma again,' she tried to whisper, but Datiqin could not hear her anymore.

Ma

Ma had never seen real mountains before but now she was in total awe. Holding on to Ming's hand, she looked at the rocks that were gliding past. The train journey was amazing, first along Lake Geneva and then up into the mountains. The last bit on a small red train — Chairman Mao would love it, Ma thought, leaning out of the window, breathing in the amazingly fresh air. On the seat opposite them sat a couple with heavy rucksacks, ropes and ice picks. How weird, Ma thought. When, finally, they got off the train in Zermatt, they saw the Matterhorn in the evening glow.

'What kitsch,' Ma laughed, underwhelmed by the beauty.

Two months earlier, her dad had told her that he would have a very special birthday present for her and Ming. As an entrepreneur in his previous life, he had hidden money abroad, money that meant nothing in China, he found, and he needed to travel abroad to enjoy it, which had become impossible for him. He realised he had to utilise his wealth through his daughter who was still able to go abroad because of her fame as a cellist. Why can she not simply move abroad? he often argued. Vienna.

'The Wiener Philharmoniker do not employ any women,' Ma said. Besides, I love Shanghai and my pupils at the Conservatory. I would never leave them, Dad.'

Ming and Ma had travelled to Moscow from where they flew to Geneva. In Zermatt, they were picked up by a horse-drawn carriage of the Monte Rosa Hotel. Her father had booked the hotel as he used to spend many summers in Zermatt and knew the family of the owners. Mr Seiler, the current host, greeted them at the hotel's magnificent entrance as their suitcases and the cello were lifted from the carriage. The sunshine was intense.

'Put on a hat, otherwise your skin will get damaged,' Ming shouted over to Ma who was standing on the balcony savouring the pure air. Ma smiled at her and held her face into the sun. Even the water tasted different, she thought as she sipped from the crystal glass.

The next day the masterclass started with Pablo Casals. Ma was not a shy person but in front of Casals, her fingers were slightly shaking. Casals walked around the room as she started playing Bach's Suite No. 3. He did not interrupt. Ma finished the Prelude and looked up. Casals sat down.

'You're incredible. Technically perfect,' he said with a quiet voice. 'But your individual charisma does not shine through yet.' Ma blushed.

And then Casals started. They worked for two hours, after which Ma, exhausted, had to sleep whilst Casals continued with the next pupil.

They stayed for two weeks in the village, going for long hikes up the slopes to remote huts when not playing music. Casals even gave Ming instructions on how she should accompany in order to allow Ma to fully develop the music. Being with Casals was unimaginable bliss only her father could have thought of. Official music contacts were always with musicians in the Soviet Union.

One late afternoon they were standing high above the Gorner Glacier, having taken the Gornergrat Train to Rotenboden and followed the trail in their newly acquired mountain boots. Ma hugged Ming as both stood on top of a rock, looking down into the abyss.

'How long would it take us to fly down to the glacier?' Ma asked, as a big black crow dived past them towards the ice. It landed softly, a tiny black dot amongst the ice and stones. Ming did not say anything and through her pullover, Ma could sense her heart beating fast.

These moments were flooding through Ma's mind as she was being interrogated. They had arrested her at home. Counter-revolutionary because she played the cello and because of her father. Now she was in prison. She faced her opponent whose face showed rage. Primitive animal, she thought. Would he hit her again? Casals had told her how he had withstood the fascists. He was an unswerving believer in democracy and republicanism, also during the dark years in Spain. I can be like him, she thought, and the memories of his words gave her strength. But, where was Ming, she wondered, hoping that Ming would not have to endure the same as her. She feared that Ming would not survive the sheer brutality of her interrogators.

Early one morning, she found the door to her cell unlocked. She opened the door. She looked around and did not recognise the building. She must be on the sixth floor, at least, she thought, looking over the low wall. Not a normal prison. Downstairs was a dark alleyway. She leaned even further over to see whether any of the windows on the floors below her were lit. How would she be able to get out of here?

She had not heard the steps and only felt the firm grip. One hand grabbing her hair, the other her trousers.

'Just shut the fuck up, you counter-revolutionary scum,' a male voice hissed as she shouted for help. She tried to struggle but the grip was firm and the man was strong.

It takes an eternity, she thought whilst flying through the air. Thoughts of Ming mixed with sounds in her ear of the 'Air' of Bach. Why did she not panic? Would she be able to play Bach again? Darkness engulfed her, and she felt it strange that she would be flying for such a long time as if towards the glacier in Zermatt. If this is death, she thought, Ming will play at my funeral.

But I will miss her, she realised. I will.

Xiaofan

Xiaofan did not know Ma or Ming. She lived in the present, having arrived only in 2018 in the Xincun. Born in America and a historian by training with a PhD from Princeton University, she studied Shanghai's urban society over the last decades. The Xincun was ideal and nobody thought — or soon forgot — that she was a post-doc doing work. Alas, Xiaofan was not only a great friend of humans, but equally attracted to the feline population of the Xincun and to Jing Zhang in particular. But as her job was that of an historian rather than a biologist, she had to concentrate on fellow humans and decided to make an exhibition showing the lives of many of the Xincun inhabitants. Their real-life stories were fascinating. Many people, including the Communist big-wigs, attended the exhibition — it was a huge success. In the end, it was clear that she knew more about each individual than each individual knew about him or herself (or the respective — even if not always respected — neighbours for that matter).

Soon her book will appear and it will be a reflection of the real people of the Xincun, of Xuhui, of her many friends. Xiaofan will say nothing at all about the characters in this book. There won't be any reference to Ma, Ming, Datiqin, Zhong, Xiaomu, Chen, Donghai, Muyang, Mrs and Comrade Bo, General Li, his granddaughter Liqin, Lanfen or Laowen. The only thing her world and the world of this book have in common is Jing Zhang. He exists and, of course, he understands German and appreciates Heidegger and Goethe.

Jing Zhang

Jing Zhang walked with them as Xiaofan and her partner schlepped their luggage from their flat to the gate. Laowen had told him that they were leaving China. Jing Zhang felt miserable and empty. With whom would he smoke cigars? He jumped onto one of the big suitcases, putting his paws on Xiaofan's legs. He looked at both of them with sad eyes. The taxi arrived, and they loaded the luggage. Datiqin said goodbye and walked off. Jing Zhang wanted to be the last one they hugged.

He was.

Long after the red lights of the taxi had disappeared into the distance of the road, Jing Zhang was still sitting on the saddle of the Mobike parked at the entrance of the Xincun. He felt too sad to move. From the distance he could hear the Beatles' music coming from Comrade Bo's House.

When the music stopped, he slowly climbed down from the Mobike to walk over to Xiaomu's place. From all he had observed over the years, Jing Zhang was not too sure whether humans would ever learn from their mistakes.

He needed a cuddle, he thought.

Postscript

April 2023. After months of the coronavirus lockdown, chaos and hardship, life suddenly went back to normal in the Xincun in early 2023. Even during lockdown, Jing Zhang had continued spending his days with Laowen and Datiqin, listening to Heidegger and Bach.

Jing Zhang learned about Comrade Bo's death at the end of November 2022. At the beginning of Covid-19, Bo had volunteered to help in the Bureau for Public Health. But he caught the virus in the autumn of 2022 and was rushed to hospital where he soon fell into a coma and never woke up.

Many had disliked Comrade Bo. Jing Zhang thought he had hated him. But his death hit everyone nonetheless. The Xincun was in shock and full of sympathy for Mrs Bo. Some were ashamed.

Every evening, on his trot to Laowen, Jing Zhang would stop and glance at the lonely shape of Mrs Bo standing at the window, looking out into the empty distance, smoking a cigarette in silence.

Strawberry fields forever, Jing Zhang thought, realising he felt sorry for her as he observed her hand, which was slightly shaking.

Acknowledgements

The author wishes to thank Jing Zhang, who made him feel welcome in the Xincun on the first day of his arrival and introduced him to all the people in this book. He met with Jing Zhang again in early 2024, and it was a most touching reunion. The first flowers had come out in the Xincun and we sat on a bench, talking about life, our common friends, Bach's cello suites and the teachings of President Xi — which he had, of course, read.

'Alas, less is more,' he observed, looking pensively into the distance, inhaling the smoke of my Cohiba cigar.

'Deng said that?' I asked.

'No, Mies van der Rohe.'

I felt humbled by his wisdom.